Dragon Stones

Book One of the Dragon Stone Saga

Author: Kristian Alva

Defiant Press
Elk Grove, CA

The Dragon Stone Saga

Book One: Dragon Stones
Book Two: The Return of the Dragon Riders
Book Three: Vosper's Revenge

The Chronicles of Tallin

Book One: The Balborite Curse (2013)
Book Two: TBA
Book Three: TBA

ISBN: 978-1-937361-00-6

Cover illustration: Jesse-lee Lang, Dark Geometry Studios

Editor: Isaac Sweeney

Find out more about the author at her official website: *www.KristianAlva.com*

Printed in the United States of America

Dedicated to my son,

the sweetest little dragon of all.

Durn

Dragon Stones

Prologue

Dragon Hunters

The mountain air was chilly, and the sun had already set. Rosy light filled the valley as dusk settled on the mountainside. Thirteen men crouched warily in the low brush. These men were used to waiting outside these mountain caves. They whispered quietly only when necessary. They were there on the direct order of Emperor Vosper, trained specifically for this purpose. These men were dragon hunters.

Dragon hunters always travel with an apprentice mage who is proficient in protection spells. These hunters were protected by a powerful masking spell, which allowed them to get close to a dragon's cave without the adult dragons detecting their smell. The young mage, Dirkla, was pale with strain—he had been holding the spell for two days without sleep, and he could not hide his fatigue.

So close to this birthing cave, even the slightest mistake could mean their doom. Captain Kathir cast another worried glance at the mage, who was shivering with exhaustion. Kathir knew that the mage's spell would eventually falter, but he would collapse before he would admit any fatigue.

That's just the way the emperor's wizards were taught—never show any sign of weakness. Kathir frowned, but he didn't voice his concerns to the mage. All wizards were a foolish, stubborn bunch. The spell was designed to keep them from being discovered, but it didn't protect them from cold and hunger. All of the men were feeling the effects of the long surveillance. They were stretched to the limit.

Kathir was exhausted, but he could not afford to go back to the emperor empty-handed. Vosper was cruel when displeased. Kathir was a mercenary, not a villain. Dragon hunting was a job like any other, except that it was dangerous and paid extremely well. Kathir had seen over thirty winters, which made him the oldest in his troop. Thirty was old for a mercenary, and even older for a dragon hunter.

Kathir was stocky and tightly muscled, with deep scars on both cheeks—the flesh merchant's mark. It was a sign that he had once been a slave. The scars were deep, but faded with age. Not all merchants marked their slaves because any mutilation lowered their value, but it made them much easier to recover if they escaped. Kathir never discussed his past with his men, and none of them ever asked.

He steadied his gaze again on the cave's entrance. His patience was rewarded. At that moment, three adult female dragons lumbered to the edge of the cave. They waddled out awkwardly, muscles stiff from months of inactivity as they guarded their eggs. Dragons' bodies were built for flight, rather than scrabbling around on the ground. Their caution had limited their flying unless absolutely necessary. They didn't want to draw any attention to their birthing cave.

These females were all carnelian dragons, the most common type. Carnelians were small, with brownish-red scales, and slightly larger than a horse. Their size made them fast and cunning. They breathed fire and had limited magical powers, just like all dragons. In the dusky light, Kathir could barely make out the brownish stone embedded at the base of their throats. All dragons produced a dragon gem as soon as they gained their ability to breathe fire—usually at about six months of age.

The stones grew in naturally, like teeth, developing to about the size of a chicken's egg. Their scales were still soft at that age, and the stone erupted at the base of the throat where it remained until the dragon died or was killed. The dragons used the stones to focus their powers, store magical energy, and communicate with their riders (if they had one).

None of the nesting females was bound to a rider; it was easy to see because none of their dragon stones were carved with the crest of a rider. Their throat stones were all smooth.

These dragons were wild.

Dragons were solitary creatures and preferred to raise their young alone, but the remaining dragon females had grown wary and now banded together in groups of two or three. The females shuffled quietly to the edge of the ridge and scanned the horizon. Their ruddy scales flickered as they stretched their wings to the sky.

These remote mountains offered better protection from dragon hunters, but little to eat, and all of the females looked very thin, their ribs plainly visible. The females, driven by hunger, decided to risk a group hunt. All three females unfurled their brown wings and took flight. The men waited anxiously. This was the moment they had been waiting for. As soon as all the females disappeared in the distance, the men ran to the cave's mouth.

The mage closed his eyes and stretched out his hands, murmuring a simple spell. The soldiers tensed, ready to retreat if necessary. "All of the females have left," the mage gasped. "There are only hatchlings in the cave. Go now!"

"Go! Move! We don't have much time!" Kathir shouted.

The men rushed inside. Kathir turned to the exhausted mage.

"Dirkla, rest outside for a moment. This won't take long. Gather your strength. We will need your powers again when we leave the mountain."

The mage nodded and slumped to the ground. The soldiers streamed into the narrow cave opening and descended on the unprotected nests, systematically slaughtering the hatchlings.

The hatchlings screeched in terror. Sprays of blood splattered in wide arcs upon the cave walls. Merely weeks old, they already had a keen intelligence. They climbed out of their nests, but it was no use. Far off in the distance, anguished shrieks from the female adults could be heard. All dragons can communicate telepathically, but these hatchlings could do little more than send a final dying plea to their mothers. The adults circled back, but none of the females arrived back in time to save their young.

The men continued to slash at the nests, careful to avoid the hatchlings' sharp teeth. A dragon bite was a foul wound, even from a hatchling. Kathir walked briskly from one end of the cave to the other, making sure that all of the hatchlings were dead. In the back of the cave lay a white dragon—the rarest of them all. It was the only white dragon he had ever seen; it had already grown twice as large as any of the others.

"How many?" barked the captain. "The emperor wants a complete count."

"Sixteen, Captain. Thirteen carnelian, two emerald, and one diamond white. This bugger put up a real fight."

The soldier kicked the dead white hatchling with his foot. It was beautiful, even in death, its iridescent mother-of-pearl scales sparkling.

The captain nodded. "Let's get moving."

Emperor Vosper would be pleased. The talons of the diamond dragon would fetch a great price.

"Move fast, all of you! Cut those talons and let's get out of here! The females will be back any moment!" barked the captain. His right cheek was scratched and the wound was already beginning to swell. "These hatchlings were aggressive. We waited too long to raid this nest."

He put a finger up to his swollen eye. A hatchling's talon had scraped his face and his eyelid. He was lucky; his eye was unharmed. Dirkla would tend to the wound once they were at a safe distance. Still, it would leave a scar, another one to add to his collection.

"We had to wait for all the females to leave, Captain. They get more cautious every season."

"Aye," agreed the captain. "They're getting better at evading us."

The men gathered the bloody talons into a mesh bag. It was proof of their kills, and each one meant a bonus from the emperor. The men walked outside, but one man stayed behind, cutting scales from the white hatchling.

"Coltrim! Get out of there—the females will be back soon. Leave that dead hatchling alone. We'll be back for the adults next month," Kathir warned while he ushered his men out of the cave. "We cannot wait for you."

"Captain, these scales will fetch a good price in the marketplace! I'll be just a minute," the man called out over his shoulder to his captain, hurriedly stuffing his pack with dragon scales.

"Your greed will get you killed, you fool," Kathir muttered under his breath.

Outside the cave, Kathir lifted the exhausted mage up to his feet and slapped his cheeks to rouse him. "Dirkla, Dirkla! Wake up!" Kathir shook him. "Focus! We need your powers again. Cast your spell while we leave the mountain. The females will be looking for us at any moment."

The mage sighed and lifted his hands, and immediately a shimmering fog enveloped them. They started down the mountainside in the moonlight, hidden by the fog and a masking spell.

A few minutes later, the enraged females touched down at the entrance of the cave. The greedy soldier was exiting, his rucksack bulging with the white scales of the dead white hatchling. The females screeched in fury, and the soldier's cries resonated down the mountainside. Coltrim would suffer a long time before he died.

Kathir did not look back.

Part One: The Discovery

Family Secrets

Elias ran towards the town square, carrying a glass jar filled with green herbs. He needed to deliver them before nightfall. Elias' grandmother, Carina, was the town midwife, and she had a vast knowledge of herbal remedies. Today he was an errand boy, delivering remedies and other concoctions all over the village.

Elias reached the shopkeeper's back door and knocked quietly. The shopkeeper, Flint Graywick, was a protective father. He was also a widower and Birla was his only child. Birla had been visiting Carina in secret in order to alleviate her painful monthly cycle. The herbs would help lessen her discomfort. In the past, Elias would have been embarrassed to discuss these things, but he had been training as an apprentice healer for years. He was used to explaining things that would make other boys embarrassed.

"I'm coming!" said a young woman from inside the shop.

Elias heard footsteps and some more chatter as Birla finished speaking to the customer inside. Birla opened the door a few minutes later. "Hi, Elias!" She was a plump girl with reddish hair. She smiled and lowered her voice to a whisper. "Do you have the medicine?"

"Yes, here it is. My grandmother gave you some extra." Elias held out the unmarked jar, which the girl pocketed in her apron.

"Thanks. I don't want my father to know. He has enough on his mind without having to worry about my little troubles."

She smiled awkwardly. All the women in the village felt comfortable talking to Elias about their aches and pains because they were used to seeing him with his grandmother. They made the rounds together to all the females in the village.

Elias dutifully rattled off the instructions. "This will be enough for three months, even if you take it every day. The jar must be kept in a cool, dark place, or the herbs will lose their power. Don't steep the herbs in boiling water. When you prepare the infusion, the water should be hot, but not boiling. Steep the herbs for at least ten minutes, but not more than thirty, or the tea will be too strong and it will cause stomach cramps. Take the tea once per day, and four times per day during your moon cycle. It will ease your pain."

"Thank you." Birla smiled again, her hand drifting down to touch the precious jar in her pocket. "Wait a minute, I have something for you!" She disappeared back into the shop. A few moments later, she emerged again with a paper-wrapped parcel. "Here. This is for you and your grandmother. Hide it under your tunic, and don't let anyone see!"

Elias took the package and slipped it under his cloak. It was fresh mutton, which was a rare treat at this time of year. It was his grandmother's payment for the herbs.

Elias ran home, clutching the precious meat to his chest. In the distance, he could see three young men coming back from a hunt. They had spent the entire day in Darkmouth Forest chasing game. Their hands were empty. Elias ducked behind a shed and crouched down near the woodpile. He could not afford anyone catching him with the meat—some of these men were desperate to feed their own families. His grandmother had been feeling weak for many months and this meat would give her strength. As they passed, Elias overheard them talking about the hunt.

"What a miserable day. Tomorrow I'll hunt rabbit. It will be easier to bring something home." It was Alafarr, the son of the town's mayor. He was as skilled a hunter as any, and it was rare for him to return empty-handed.

This year had been difficult and many villagers were going hungry. Blight and rain had ruined many crops, and game was scarce. Even the wealthier members of the village were having trouble keeping their families fed. If Alafarr was actually hunting for food and not sport, then things were terrible indeed.

23

"We'll try again at dawn," said Fastaor, who was Alfarr's cousin. "Let's travel deeper into the forest next time, perhaps for a few days. Together, we'll catch something. I set some snares this afternoon, so we might get lucky tonight."

"This season has been abysmal," complained Galmor, who was Fastaor's brother and the youngest of the group. "The grain is stunted, the corn has blight, and the forest has nothing for us to eat. Does the emperor expect us to eat rats?"

Fastaor struck the back of Galmor's head with his bow staff.

"Owww!" cried Galmor, rubbing the top of his skull.

"Shut up, you fool! Vosper's spies are everywhere, and men have been killed for less. Instead of complaining, say a prayer to the hunting goddess tonight. May she guide our arrows tomorrow, or else we'll starve."

Galmor grumbled, but he did not argue further with his older brother. He knew Fastaor was right. To criticize the emperor openly was blasphemy, and even in a remote mountain village like Persil, it was still prudent to avoid provoking the emperor's wrath.

The men passed by Elias' hiding place, their shoulders hunched. No one had brought home anything larger than a rabbit for weeks. Elias felt sorry for them, but he also knew that the men were too proud to gather mushrooms and tubers, believing it beneath them. Elias had no such prejudices, and it was this way that he and his grandmother always had enough to eat.

Elias stayed hidden until the men were out of sight. Then he crawled out from his hiding place and sprinted the rest of the way home, careful that he wasn't followed.

He arrived at his grandmother's cottage out of breath. As he opened the door, he could smell the pungent odor from her vast collection of herbs. Bottles lined every shelf.

His grandmother was making dinner. A black pot boiled on the hearth, waiting for his return. She had already filled the pot with cut-up potatoes, onions, and garlic—anything they had in the cellar. The smell of the hearty soup was filled the small cabin with a wonderful aroma. His grandmother was resting on her bed.

The tiny cottage only had two rooms: the kitchen and Elias' bedroom. Elias rarely slept in his room—it was simply too cold. Carina slept in the kitchen near the hearth, and she had always done so. Elias often slept near the fire as well—it was warmer and he felt safer watching his grandmother during the night, especially since she had fallen ill. Elias went to his grandmother's bedside. She had dozed off.

"Grandmother…" He shook her shoulder gently. "I have the meat."

Carina's shoulder-length hair was shock white. She wore it in a loose bun at the base of her neck, with a patterned fabric kerchief tied in the back, covering her head and ears. The vibrant colors of the kerchief made her skin look even paler than usual.

Her eyelids fluttered open. "Ah, Elias. Good…you're here. Go bolt the door, and give me the parcel."

Elias rushed to the door, sliding the lock. Then he reached under his cloak and pulled out the precious bundle, handing it to his grandmother. She opened it and frowned, inspecting the pieces of mutton by turning them over with her index finger. "Tsk! This is from an older animal—the meat will need to boil for a long time."

"But Grandmother, there's a nice chunk of fat and a big bone filled with marrow; that's good. It will strengthen us both."

Carina smiled and touched his cheek. "Ever the optimist, eh? Yes, I suppose you're right. Beggars can't be choosers. Put it in the soup pot; it will make a good meal for us tonight and the next day."

She handed the package back to Elias and closed her eyes again, falling back onto the pillow. The small effort tired her.

Elias frowned. His grandmother's strength was fading. Although her healing knowledge was vast, she could not turn back time. She was an old woman, one of the oldest in the village. Her health continued to deteriorate. He wished he could do more to help her.

Elias walked to the fireplace and dropped all of the mutton and chunks of fat into the pot, stirring the broth and vegetables. His stomach grumbled, but he knew that the rich stew would be worth the wait.

Elias turned around and noticed that Carina was watching him intently.

"I thought you were asleep. Why don't you rest and I'll wake you when the soup is ready?" asked Elias.

"I feel fine. I had a nap earlier." Carina patted the bed. "Elias, come sit next to me. I want to tell you a story."

This was their nightly routine. Carina would tell him a story, and then they would eat and go to bed. Usually, she talked about healing magic, but sometimes she would tell fantastic stories about cities she had visited, people she had met, and journeys she had taken. Sometimes, if Elias was lucky, she would talk about the dragons.

"Elias, I am old. I may not see another sun cycle."

Elias hung his head. He didn't argue. He knew it was true. Every year she seemed more fragile.

"You're a good boy, and I have been blessed to have you by my side for all these years. I have taught you everything I know about healing. I'm sorry I could not teach you more. It is woman's magic, and I know that you've been ridiculed by the other boys."

"Grandmother, it's not that bad, really. They don't tease me so much."

"I did the best I could, and I taught you a useful skill. You have a potent gift—much more powerful than mine. It will help you in times of trouble. One day you'll understand that. Hopefully, you'll get lucky and learn how to focus your powers even more."

Elias spent his younger years collecting herbs and learning healing lore while all the other boys learned how to hunt. The others also teased him for being "fatherless." Elias' mother and father had died during the war, and Carina had raised him. Elias enjoyed learning magic, but he hated being bullied.

The teasing lessened a year ago when Elias stumbled on an older boy who had broken his leg in the forest. It was Shamus, one of the boys who tormented Elias the most. Shamus had fallen off a rocky outcropping. It was

27

late afternoon and very hot, and by the time Elias found him, Shamus was delirious with pain and thirst. Elias ran to him and saw the bone of his right leg poking out of the skin.

"Shamus, Shamus, can you hear me?"

The boy moaned, drifting in and out of consciousness. Elias squeezed his leg and Shamus yelled, *"Auggggh!"*

"There! That got your attention. Shamus, it's Elias." Elias slapped his face lightly. "Wake up! Drink this."

Elias lifted his water skin to Shamus' mouth. Shamus moaned again. His lips were cracked, and foamy spittle had formed at the corners. He drank deeply from the waterskin.

"Elias? I—I fell chasing a stag. I've been here all day, screaming for help." His voice croaked. Elias looked up and saw the rocky ledge far above.

"You're lucky you're not dead. You should say a prayer to the healing goddess for your good fortune," said Elias. "Don't worry, I'll help you."

"I-I can't walk. I tried to pick myself up, but I can't bear any weight on this leg."

"I know it hurts, but I have to set your leg, or you'll never get out of here. I'm going to find you some herbs to dull the pain, and then I'll splint your leg. I need to go search for supplies. Here, take this," Elias said, handing Shamus his waterskin.

Shamus grabbed Elias' tunic. "You won't be long?"

"I'll work as fast as I can. I promise. Soon you'll be back home in your own bed. Don't worry." Elias patted his hand, copying the behavior that he had seen his grandmother use hundreds of times over the years.

After a few minutes, Elias returned. "Here, chew on this. It's numbweed. It tastes bitter, but it will dull your pain so I can set your bone."

Shamus chewed the purple weed with a grimace. "It tastes awful. Do I swallow it?"

"Just chew the leaves and swallow the juice. Tuck the herb into your cheek until the bitter flavor goes away. Spit out the plant or else your stomach will ache. Your body can't digest the plant fibers."

Elias prepared the branches and the twine. His palms glowed faintly as he tied the vines together, casting a simple spell upon the splint, so that the branches would straighten and hold. He whispered the spell under his breath, careful not to let Shamus overhear his words in the old tongue.

"I'm already starting to feel better," Shamus said.

"Good. That means the numbweed is working. Now we must fix your leg. I'm sorry, but this is going to hurt, even with the numbweed." He took a leather strap from his pack and doubled it over, handing it to Shamus. "Bite down on this. I'm going to set the break. Close your eyes."

He waited until Shamus closed his eyes. "Now take a deep breath." Elias grasped the broken limb firmly with both hands. Muttering the old language under his breath, Elias said a healing spell and prepared to set the bone. Shamus groaned in pain when Elias touched his leg, and screamed when the bones snapped back into place.

"Holy Baghra! That hurt. I'm seeing spots," said Shamus, exhaling deeply.

Elias knew that the spell would work quickly. The bones were already knitting together under the skin. Shamus would be able to walk with a crutch, which was enough to get him out of the forest.

"There—that's good. Now I'm going to put two forked saplings on either side of your leg and bind them with vines. You'll be able to walk slowly. You can lean on me. I'll bear your weight on this side, and we'll walk back to the village together."

Elias offered Shamus his hand and pulled the injured boy up. Shamus touched the injured leg to the ground and winced. It was painful, but he could bear weight on it.

"Thank you," said Shamus in a trembling voice. Tears and sweat poured down his face, but he was smiling. He knew the worst was over.

"Don't thank me yet. We have a long way to go before we're out of this forest."

Elias helped him walk, and they hobbled back to the village slowly. They had to stop and rest frequently, so it was close to midnight when they finally reached the outskirts of the village. A search party had gathered at the forest's edge. Some of the men held torches. They all looked anxious.

"Shamus left before dawn this morning! Where could he be? He's never stayed in the forest this long! He'll never survive the night—he didn't even take a cloak. He's just wearing a tunic." Shamus' mother wrung her hands in fear.

Just then, the boys came into view. Shamus was limping, with the much smaller Elias supporting him.

"Mother!" Shamus called out, and the men looked up, surprised. The villagers rushed to meet them. Shamus' mother pushed past the men to embrace her son.

"Shamus! I was so worried. What happened to you?"

"I fell, Mother—chasing a deer. Elias... he found me. He fixed my leg and saved me."

Shamus' mother grabbed Elias in a grateful embrace. She kissed his cheek. "Thank you, Elias!"

"An impressive rescue, young man!" the men shouted, slapping Elias on the back. Elias smiled. He was tired but appreciative of all the attention. No one ever fussed over him like this.

Shamus' older brother stepped in and helped carry Shamus the rest of the way home.

Word of the rescue spread. Shamus' mother even baked Elias a sweet pastry. After that, no one really teased Elias anymore.

"Elias? Elias? Are you listening to me?" Carina flicked Elias' hand.

Her gentle reprimand startled him out of the day-dream. "Yes, I'm sorry, Grandmother. I'm listening."

"Tonight, we must wait a long time for the lamb to cook, so I'm going to tell you an old story. You're almost a man. Soon you'll see your sixteenth cycle, and it's time that you understand our land's history." Carina's voice dropped to a whisper. "Most are afraid to speak of it because they dread the emperor's wrath, but I am an old woman and I have little to fear."

"Grandmother, don't speak like that. It's bad luck," said Elias, frowning.

"Bah! What have I to fear? The emperor can do nothing to me here. We're far from his opulent palace, full of slaves and lizard bones! He ignores our people while they starve, so he can collect more dragon trophies for his walls."

It was rare for Carina to speak this way. Among her limited magical gifts was the gift of sight, and she felt darkness spreading across the land. Elias felt it, too. People were more guarded, more frightened. But of what? No one could say for sure.

"Elias, when I was a girl, children with magical gifts were highly prized. Mageborns were sent to train in the capital city. From a very young age, they trained as apprentice mages. When my parents discovered my magical gifts, I was only twelve. I had started my moon's cycle the previous month. That is when the magical gifts usually become obvious—after a boy or girl goes through their Changing Time.

"Our family had a pet—an orange cat named Farris. I adored him. One day, some boys threw rocks at Farris and crushed his pelvis. Farris dragged himself home to me on two legs, mewling in pain.

"I found him, his fur caked with dirt and blood. Broken bones poked through the skin. I cried into his fur and said prayers to the goddess of healing. But I didn't know any real spells, and my powers were weak. My palms started to glow, but I couldn't save Farris. I was only able to relieve his pain and stop the bleeding."

"So what happened?"

"Farris simply went to sleep and died two days later. I gave him a painless death. It was all that I could do.

That was many, many moons ago. My parents discussed my magical gift for weeks. Most parents would have sent me immediately to the Temple to train—they would have received a nice dowry for me, and it's best to start training as soon as a child's gift is discovered. But my father was already a wealthy merchant, and our family had no need for the mage dowry. My mother—your great-grandmother—didn't want me to leave.

"I was very spoiled. I lived a life without troubles or worries." She glanced away for a moment, overcome by emotion.

Elias looked up. Carina rarely talked about her childhood or her parents. A shadow of pain crossed her face. Then she sighed and carried on. "My own grandmother also had the mageborn gift, and she was a powerful healer in her own time."

"Why did your parents wait so long to start your training?"

"At first, they wanted me to celebrate my coming-of-age ceremony. It was an important rite of passage for young girls back then, with feasting that could last for days. It's rarely celebrated now because most families can't afford to spend money on such luxuries. In the end, though, my parents had little choice. A few years later, Vosper took the throne and the countryside was no longer safe. My parents felt that they couldn't send me to train in Aonach—they were terrified of the emperor and his increasing powers. My mother's premonition was correct. The following year, Vosper assassinated his own father and became the emperor."

"What happened after Vosper took the throne?" asked Elias. "Was there a war?"

"No, not at first. Vosper was ruthless, but shrewd. He never declared war against anyone. He used assassins and dark magic to secure his position. First he slaughtered his four brothers. Not all at once—but they all died under suspicious circumstances. Then Vosper took control of Aonach Tower, under the guise that he was 'protecting' the mages. He killed any spellcasters who refused to serve him, branding them as traitors. Then he sent soldiers out to scour the countryside for any other mageborns—even children. All mages were sent to the palace under guard. They were forced to pledge fealty to the emperor, or they were executed. Vosper transferred the most powerful mages to his palace and refocused all their magical training on his own defense."

"How did you escape?"

"Many of the weaker spellcasters escaped detection. The emperor subjugated the strongest mages when he stormed Aonach, but more than a few of us escaped enslavement. My magical gifts are limited, so I never attracted any suspicion. Some mages can only cast a few spells—enough to survive. There will always be spellcasters—it's impossible to eradicate us all.

"I was one of the fortunate ones. I was still young and not many people knew about my gift. Keeping me hidden saved my life. We fled the city and changed our family name. Luckily, Father had saved some money. Those were difficult times."

"If you fled the city, how did you receive your training?" asked Elias.

"My parents risked everything to send me to Miklagard, the last outpost of the free mages. Miklagard was a poor substitute for Aonach Tower. Only a handful of Masters escaped—those who were traveling away from Aonach during the emperor's attack. I only trained at Miklagard for five years. Before the war, parents received a mage dowry for their children. Now, mages are forced to charge fees for training. There were many mageborns who were more powerful than I, but could not afford to train."

"What did you learn in Miklagard?"

"I learned herb-lore and how to read simple spells. The Masters discovered early on that I had a gift for healing. I also learned how to hide my gift. Most people just assume that I'm an excellent midwife. Those who suspect rarely ask questions. A few times, though, I got careless and my magical gift was exposed. Twice I've had to leave a village because I feared that I would be reported to the emperor. It's hard to believe that Vosper would be interested in a feeble mage like me, but you never know. It pays to be cautious. It's a mistake to underestimate the treachery and greed of your neighbors."

It was rare for Carina to reveal so much family history at once, and it was obvious that she struggled with the memories, still so painful after all these years.

"I'm thankful for my gift and my teaching. It has allowed me to earn a living while so many others have starved. After the destruction of the Temple, most believed that the emperor was satisfied. But Vosper had much higher aspirations than just controlling the mages of Durn. Two years later, he assassinated the Five Kings, charging them all with high treason. Everyone knew that it was a ploy for Vosper to take control of the entire continent."

"Grandmother, I thought one of the kings survived," said Elias. "What about King Mitca?"

"Yes... the rebel king. Who could forget about him? Unfortunately for the emperor, Mitca *did* survive. During the war, he was merely a prince. Mitca was the crown prince of Ravenwood and the only male child of King Galain. The prince survived because Galain sacrificed his own life to save his son's. Galain discovered the emperor's plot months before because he planted a spy in the emperor's palace."

"Why didn't Galain just fight the emperor himself?"

"Galain knew that he wasn't strong enough to stand up against all of Vosper's armies and his corrupt wizards. Instead, Galain disguised his son as a beggar and whisked him out of the city with a few of his honor guard. Those men had guarded Mitca since his infancy and, to this day, the surviving members are fiercely loyal to the prince. Galain stayed in the city. A slave boy posed as a decoy for the prince. The city was captured shortly thereafter and the entire royal family was put to death."

"Vosper didn't realize that the slave boy was a fake?"

"No. Galain killed himself and the boy in a staged suicide the night before their official executions. The deception was perfect. It was many years before Vosper discovered Galain's trickery. By then, Mitca had already settled in the Death Sands and established the rebel Kingdom of Parthos. Vosper's overconfidence cost him the rule of the continent. Now Parthos is a thorn in his side that will never go away, and every year Mitca grows stronger."

"Why doesn't the emperor just attack Parthos?"

"Oh, he has tried! He has tried! But Vosper has failed again and again. The Death Sands are almost impossible to cross, and the kingdom is heavily guarded. Parthos is a huge, well-populated city. The majority of its inhabitants are tribesmen, and they are inherently distrustful of the emperor. Parthos has a majestic fortress, which is carved right into the mountainside. It even has its own water source, an underground spring that can sustain the entire city if necessary. Mitca has his own mages, and the free mages of Miklagard are his allies. King Mitca is the emperor's only real adversary. Plus... Mitca offered refuge to the last of the dragon riders." Carina whispered the last sentence under her breath.

"Dragon riders? I thought they were all dead!" said Elias.

"Quiet! Keep your voice down!"

"Sorry, Grandmother."

"The emperor is lying. There are still dragon riders. No one knows how many survive—even the nomads who live in the desert refuse to say. The desert people know how to keep secrets. The riders have sworn to protect Mitca, and the Kingdom of Parthos is their last sanctuary."

"King Mitca is not the emperor's only enemy. What about Balbor Island?" asked Elias.

"Ah, yes. Balbor, the Island of Death. The inhabitants of Balbor don't pledge their allegiance to the emperor, but they're not Vosper's enemies. They're independent. The Balborites are mercenaries. Unlike the rest of Durn, priests rule the island, not kings. They control their people with their foul religion, through bloody offerings and dark magic."

The old woman leaned in close to her nephew's ear. "Balbor is truly cursed—it is bad luck even to speak of it. Very little is known of their rituals. Some folktales tell us that the firstborn child of every female is dismembered as an offering to their dark god. They're a secretive people and have been so for an eternity. Centuries ago, the Balborites sealed off their only port city. It is impossible to come or go to that forsaken place. If any ship attempts to land on the coastline, their priests destroy it."

"But you said the Balborites were mercenaries? How do they survive? How do they get supplies?"

"No one really knows. The only people who ever leave the island are trained assassins. They leave alone by boat to commit their murders and also report information back to the priests. Balborite assassins command a high price because they're all mageborn and highly skilled. They practice death magic, foul magic. They're the most ruthless killers in all of Durn, murdering without remorse or regret. They simply work for the highest bidder. Even though Balbor is not part of the emperor's kingdom, Vosper would be foolish to try and conquer it. Balbor is the island of blackness, a place so full of wickedness that even our greedy emperor does not desire it. He is satisfied to let them be."

Just then, Elias' stomach grumbled. His hand flew to his midsection, embarrassed by the noise.

"Listen to me, carrying on like a senile old woman!" Carina laughed. "Of course, you're hungry. Check the stew.

It should be ready. Ladle yourself a bowl and bring me the marrow bone. We will share it. Tonight, we don't go hungry." They ate the delicious stew and prepared for bed.

That night, Elias dreamt of dragons, which he had never seen except in pictures. He was walking in the forest, and he could see them silhouetted against the night sky. Their scales glittered in the moonlight. One of the dragons touched down right next to him and reached out its clawed hand towards him. Startled, Elias ran into the safety of the underbrush. The dragon gave chase, bellowing in fury. He ran as fast as he could, jumping over rocks and brush. His side burned.

Eventually, he fell, careening face-first into the damp earth, his breath coming in ragged gasps. When he turned around, the dragon was gone. He was alone in the forest. It was the first of many dreams that he would have about dragons.

Discoveries

Elias awoke before dawn and dressed himself in the dark. Carina slept, her chest rising and falling gently. Elias went to her bedside and tucked the quilt under her chin. She looked pale.

Last night, Carina had given Elias a list of wild mushrooms to gather, so that was his task for today. Some of the mushrooms were rare and would be difficult to find. He ate a light breakfast, filled his waterskin, and packed his rucksack with a chunk of cooked lamb and some bread. Then he left the cabin, walking quickly.

The sky was clear and the air was icy cold. It had drizzled the night before, and everything was covered with a thin layer of frost. Elias slipped his hands into his pockets and continued to walk deeper into Darkmouth Forest. The walking soon warmed him up, and it wasn't long before he was sweating underneath his cloak. It was beautiful here—

so peaceful. Other boys rarely went so deep into the forest. Most hunted close to the forest's edge. Early on, Elias escaped the village bullies by coming here. He knew how to navigate the forest, and he wasn't scared to travel farther than a day's walk. Elias had never found anything to fear here. In fact, it was one of the places where he felt the most at home.

He knew from Carina's maps that the northern part of the forest ended at the Elburgian Mountains. The longest he'd ever spent in the forest was two days, and he'd gotten an earful from his grandmother when he returned.

By mid-afternoon, he had reached a secluded clearing that he knew well. There was a natural spring on the left, surrounded by a circle of oak trees. On the right, there was a mound of rotted logs. Every type of mushroom and fungus grew here, fed by the moist air and decaying wood. Soon Elias was gathering tiny red-capped mushrooms and collecting them into a mesh bag, being careful not to smash them in the process.

They needed to be kept intact until he got back to the cottage where Carina would sort and dry them. Even though he enjoyed being in the forest, collecting mushrooms was a tedious business. It was too cold to take a quick dip in the pond, but he could feel the sweat running down his back as he bent down over and over to harvest the tiny mushrooms.

By the time he finished filling the bag, he was tired and hungry.

I'll just eat my lunch and hurry back home, he thought. *It will be cold out here after the sun sets, and I don't want to get stuck if it starts to snow.*

Blooming winter flowers, especially lilies, grew everywhere. Elias noticed an unusual number of bees collecting pollen in the clearing. There seemed to be so many that he suspected there was a new hive right in the clearing. Wild honey was difficult to find, and even more so in the winter. *Maybe I'll get lucky and find some honeycomb. That would be a rare treat for us.* He observed the bees for some time, and he was rewarded when he saw the opening to a beehive in a nearby tree.

What a stroke of luck! If I can come back with some honey, Grandmother will be delighted, he thought.

Elias set to work on a smoke stick. He stripped a sturdy branch of its leaves, and then wrapped the end of with some dried bark and grass. Then he rolled the end in pitch.

He crawled up the tree slowly, glad that there were only a few dozen bees at the mouth of the hive. Even when calmed by smoke, the bees were still dangerous, so Elias put on his hood and wrapped a piece of cloth tightly around his face, leaving only a slit for his eyes. He whispered a short spell under his breath, and the end of the stick caught on fire. It burned with a greasy black smoke.

Elias jammed the smoke stick into the opening. The effect was immediate, and the bees started to stumble around the hive. Perfect. The hive was small—about arm's reach into the tree trunk. He could smell the delicious scent of wild honey. There was also something strange—a piece of the honeycomb looked green, as if something had grown into it. He grabbed his knife and cut combs from the hive, moving fast to avoid being stung. Bees swarmed on his cloak, and as he removed the precious honeycomb, a bee landed on his thumb and stung him.

"Ow! Sweet Baghra, that hurt!"

He jumped down from the tree, running a safe distance while shaking off his cloak. He removed the stinger, sucking his thumb. His thumb throbbed, but it was worth it. He wrapped the honey in leaves and tucked it into his bag. His grandmother would appreciate this treat. He considered using a healing spell to stop the swelling, but decided against it. His grandmother said that sometimes it was better to just let your body heal naturally.

Elias left the clearing. The sun was low in the sky, and the air felt colder. *I must hurry or I'll be stuck here after nightfall,* he thought. Instead of walking, he ran the entire way back to Persil, and made it to the forest's edge just after sundown.

"Grandmother!" he shouted as he flew through the door. "I have a surprise for you!"

Carina was hunched over the hearth, stirring the leftovers of the previous night's stew. She seemed better today. "Elias? You're home late. Was it difficult to find the mushrooms?"

"No, I found them and filled the jar just like you asked. But look! I found a beehive. I got honey!"

"Really?" Carina's wrinkled face broke into a wide grin. "Let's see it!"

Elias pulled the broken honeycombs from his pack and unwrapped them. It was only a small amount, a bit larger than a man's fist, but it was such a rare indulgence that Carina was ecstatic.

"Oh, my lovely boy! What a marvelous treasure. I'll make some flatbread and we'll enjoy it with our leftover soup. Tonight we eat like kings!"

"I only got one sting, on my thumb." He stretched his hand out, and Carina grasped it. The right thumb was badly swollen.

"Tsk. I'll fix this for you, my dear." Carina went to her cupboard and pulled a jar off the shelf that was filled with a gooey black substance. "This will reduce the swelling and draw the poison out. Your finger will be normal by tomorrow morning." She spread a thick film on his affected thumb and wrapped Elias' hand with a clean strip of cloth. "There you go, boy."

"Thank you, Grandmother. It feels much better." It was true. The pain was almost gone, and Elias could feel the swelling going down.

"Have a seat, Elias—you've done enough work for today. I'll pour you a big bowl of stew. It will only take a minute to warm the bread." Carina went to the cupboard and took out three pieces of brown flatbread. She placed them near the fire on a flat stone.

Elias sat down near the fire, stretching his hands out. The cabin was tiny—not more than a one-room shack, but it was warm and comfortable. It felt good to be home. The soup bubbled softly, and he watched Carina ladle a giant helping into his bowl.

"There you go. Eat the soup, and I'll go spread some honey on the bread." Carina turned to the table and opened the leaves that held the honeycomb. "Tsk. One of the honeycombs has a bit of muck inside of it."

"Yes, I noticed it when I was collecting the honey, but I was in such a hurry to get out of there that I didn't remove it. It's probably fungus."

Carina dug into the comb with her fingernail and pulled out a greenish stone, about the size of a chicken's egg.

"No! It can't be!" she screamed.

"Grandmother! What's wrong? What is it?" Elias ran to her side. Her face was white.

"It's—it's not... it's not a fungus. It's a stone. An emerald. Elias, where did you find this?"

"An emerald? Really? I wonder how it got inside the tree?"

Elias walked to the table and picked it up. The surface of the stone was carved in a negative image, like the opposite of a cameo. "Grandmother, look! It's carved into the shape of a dragon!"

"I know. It's an intaglio—a dragon rider's gem. Elias, I haven't seen anything like this in years."

"They must be very rare! We could sell this and make lots of money!" Elias' eyes glittered with excitement.

"No! Elias—you don't understand. This gem once belonged to a rider. Simply possessing this gem could have us both killed."

"But why?" asked Elias.

"Dragon stones have immense power. When a dragon is wild, the gemstone on its throat is smooth. The uncut gem is a cabochon—opaque and shiny. If a dragon accepts a rider, powerful spells are cast to bind the dragon to the rider. During the binding ceremony, the dragon's gem splits, and an image is scorched into the gem. The dragon stone is then divided in two by magic. The rider gets one half, and the other half stays embedded in the dragon's throat. That is the way it will remain until they die. The dragon and the rider are united together permanently. Their minds link and they are as one."

"I wonder how the stone ended up in Darkmouth Forest?" asked Elias, his hunger forgotten.

"It could be very old. This is not the dragon's half—this half belonged to a rider. You can tell because the image is carved *into* the stone. The half that remains with the dragon is a relief carving—a cameo. The two halves of the stone fit together—like a mold and its casting."

"If we have the stone, does it mean that this rider is dead?"

"I don't know. I'm not sure what happens after a rider or his dragon dies. If the stone is shattered, then it usually kills the rider and the dragon, too. This stone is undamaged, so I don't know if that means the rider is alive or dead. Some riders wore the stone as a pendant, but many opted to have the stone implanted permanently in their chest. That ended up being a mistake because during the war the emperor's men would merely strip off the rider's shirt to confirm their identity. If they found a rider, the emperor would kill him or her on the spot."

"Does the stone have any magical power?"

"Yes. The stone links a dragon and his rider together, and makes it possible for a rider to communicate telepathically with other dragons. A dragon and his rider can communicate as soon as they're bound together. A dragon's language is a combination of guttural sounds and telepathic images. Learning dragon tongue is extremely difficult, and it requires telepathic abilities. Some independent mages have learned how to communicate with dragons, but it took years of training. However, it is said that elves can communicate with dragons effortlessly, as they can with all creatures."

She picked up the dragon gem, sticky with honey, and traced the image with her finger. "It's beautiful, isn't it? I've never seen one up close. It's green, so it would have been from an emerald dragon. That's—that's all I know about them." She placed the stone back on the table.

"This is incredible!" Elias grabbed it and held it up to the light. "Grandmother, be reasonable. It's valuable, and we could use the money. Let's sell it to Frogar."

Frogar was the village junk merchant. Unpopular for his sour character and greed, he was also useful because he would buy almost anything—if the price was right.

"No! It's too dangerous. Frogar is a liar and a cheat. He would skin his own mother for a bag of coppers. Take it back into the forest tomorrow and put it back where you found it."

"But Grandmother..." Elias started to protest, but she shook her head.

"Do not argue with me, Elias. My decision is final. Tell no one of the stone. Take it back where you found it. We cannot risk bringing this type of attention upon us."

Carina took the stone and hid it in the cabinet, behind her bottles of herbs and remedies.

Elias hung his head, annoyed. Why let something so valuable go to waste, just because of some silly superstition?

They finished the rest of the meal in silence. Even the delicious taste of the honeyed flatbread could not improve his mood.

When he went to bed that night, Elias dreamt again of dragons. This time, a single green dragon approached him in the forest. It was twice the size of a horse, but he was not afraid. The dragon reached out to him and Elias saw the carved stone embedded in the dragon's throat. The stone was identical to the one that Elias found in the forest. The dragon's claw scratched at his throat, and Elias woke up in a cold sweat.

"Aaaaugh!" he yelled. His heart pounded. It was only a dream, he reminded himself.

Elias rolled back over and went to sleep.

Frogar, the Junk Merchant

When Elias awoke the following morning, he shivered with cold. The fire had died down during the night, and the tiny cottage seemed darker than usual. He shuddered, got up, and fed another log to the fire. He peeked outside his tiny window and saw the ground covered in snow.

Blast! The snow will make it impossible to find any food in the forest, he thought. Elias took a deep breath, snuck into the kitchen, and grabbed the dragon stone. He looked over at Carina and saw that she was still sleeping. He put the stone in a pouch and hung it around his neck.

Elias donned his warmest cloak, a thick wool garment that had once been his grandfather's. It was simple, but very well-made, and it kept him warm even on the coldest days. Carina had given it to him two years ago as a gift. He also had some leather boots and a hat that was lined with beaver fur. He hardly felt the cold as he stepped outside. The snow crunched under his feet as he walked towards the village square.

Persil wasn't a large settlement, but it bustled with activity. There were children running in the streets and farmers carting their winter harvest for sale. The village was defended by local militia, and men patrolled the village borders with simple weapons. Most of Persil's revenue came from fur trading. The hunting had been poor this year, and families were struggling.

A farmer dragged a large selection of winter squash through the street. The squash came in different sizes and colors. Some gourds were the size of a child's fist. Others were pumpkins, larger than a man's head. A few women strolled up to the farmer, haggling over price. One woman held an infant swaddled tightly in blankets, except for his mouth nursing at her breast.

Last year the pumpkin farmer would not have garnered so much attention, but this year, food was scarce. A single large pumpkin could feed a family.

"Kemril, give us a good price on your pumpkins. I want two of these big 'uns you've got here." The housewife plucked two large pumpkins from his cart.

"I can give you a good price. Them smaller squashes are sweeter and good for makin' pastry."

"Ohhh, Kemril! Who has the money to make pastry these days? No, no, these pumpkins will cook in my soup pot with water and potatoes—they'll stretch better that way. I have five mouths to feed. I don't have any coppers, but I'll trade you some butter, freshly churned this morning. All our goats are still giving milk, thank Baghra."

"All right, I'll take the butter. Come back with it and we'll trade."

It went on like this for several minutes, the village housewives haggling back and forth. Few had any coins, but all of the women wanted to trade.

Elias watched the lively exchange for a while before continuing on his way. In the village square, the cottages were built closer together. The homes were all small, painted white, and made from rock or mud brick. In the heart of the village, there was a cluster of shops. The butcher, the candlemaker, and the local glazier all ran their businesses here. Elias kept walking briskly and reached the last two homes, which were backed up against the forest. Only two structures stood in a snow-covered meadow. One was the farrier's place, and the other was Frogar's house.

Frogar was a scrap dealer. He bought all kinds of rubbish. The outside of his shop was filthy, the ground littered with garbage. The inside was even worse. Boxes stacked to the ceiling, every inch filled with empty jars, gadgets, and dusty knick-knacks. Frogar lived in squalor, but was actually quite wealthy.

Elias walked into the shop, and a little bell rang on the doorjamb announcing his arrival. After a few minutes, Frogar shuffled to the counter.

"What do you want, boy?"

His body smelled sour, like old whiskey. Frogar's cheek was stuffed with chewing tobacco, and he spat into a brass cup. Elias' nose wrinkled, and he put his hand up instinctively to hold it, but caught himself in time. He didn't want to put Frogar in a bad mood.

"I have something to sell. A jewel."

"A *jewel*, eh? What kind of jewel?"

"An emerald! And it's as big as an egg!"

"Bah! Sure it is!" Frogar frowned. "Do you think I'm a fool, boy? Blast you for waking me and wasting my time." Frogar turned and started to walk away.

"Wait! Don't leave. It's real!" Elias cried. He reached inside his tunic and pulled out the deerskin sachet.

"I don't buy river rocks," said Frogar. But he waited.

"I swear, it's real." Elias placed the little pouch on the counter, and it opened like a flower, revealing the emerald inside. "It's a dragon stone. I found it in the forest."

Frogar's eyes popped. Elias heard Frogar's quick intake of breath. Frogar was a practiced negotiator, but even he could not hide his surprise.

"Let me see it, boy." His wrinkled hand reached out to grab it.

"No!" Elias snatched it back. Frogar's eyebrows went up. "Don't touch it—I don't trust you."

The old man's eyes narrowed. "I need to touch it—to make sure that it's real. Otherwise, how can I offer you a fair price?" He leered, revealing yellowed teeth.

"I might be a boy, but I'm not a fool. You know the stone is real. If you want it, offer me a fair price right now. Otherwise, I'll travel to Jutland and sell the stone there. In Jutland, there are even greedier merchants than you!"

Frogar scowled. "Why you... little snot-nosed bugger!"

"I don't want to argue! What is your price?" Elias was starting to feel nauseated. His throat was dry, choked by the dusty air.

Frogar shook his head, and his face broke into a wicked sneer. "You're nothing but a young fool! You have no idea what you have. I don't want your dragon stone, stupid boy."

Elias' mouth dropped open. He hadn't expected that response from the old man.

"That stone is a curse. No one will buy it. Not here, not in Jutland—not anywhere. It will bring you nothing but misery. Now get out of my shop before I throw you out." His voice rose to a shriek at the end, and tobacco-laced spittle flew from his mouth.

"I-I don't believe you. I'm going to sell it and make a nice profit, you'll see!"

Elias pocketed the stone and walked back outside into the snow. He looked back and saw Frogar observing him through a filthy window. He was laughing—a cackling, unholy laugh that echoed down the road. The hair on the back of Elias' neck rose and his heart filled with fear.

Elias ran all the way home.

The Death Sands

Dozens of soldiers lined up like dominos in the desert heat. Archers patrolled the look-out towers. Parthos was a meticulously planned city, designed in layers whittled from the mountainside. The city was a fortress, with successive safety walls and defensive bulwarks. It backed up against a mountain and was surrounded by sheer cliffs on either side.

Everything in Parthos ran with a crazed efficiency that ensured its continued survival. The city was built on a natural spring that ran year-round. There was a natural oasis nearby, and it even allowed animals some limited grazing around the city perimeter.

An aqueduct system, combined with mandatory rainwater collection tanks on every roof, assured that the city's inhabitants always had enough water. The homes inside the city walls were small with flat roofs, designed to save energy. The mud-brick homes weren't much larger than sheds, but they were functional, staying cool during the day and warm during the chilly desert nights. Some citizens even lived in remote caves on the mountain, doubling as permanent look-outs. Heavily guarded underground tunnels led to catacombs stocked with provisions—the city always operated as though it was under siege.

Guardsmen stood alert at the city gates, minding their posts in silence. They rotated every hour to drink and cool down. The walls were never unattended. There were also soldiers on mounted patrol; the men rode camels instead of horses. The finest camel breeders worked in Parthos, and nomadic tribes from the Death Sands ventured there to improve their stock.

The city's camels were well-trained and suited to the dry environment. The animals could go several days without food or water and could live up to fifty years. The camels retained water so efficiently that their dung could be burned almost immediately after it was excreted. The dung was a substitute for firewood in the desert.

Camels were intelligent and fast, able to run without stopping for many leagues. The king's camel herds numbered into the thousands, supplying his people with meat, milk, and fuel.

Inside the city walls, the streets bustled with activity. Most of the inhabitants were involved in trading or smuggling, and Parthos was recognized for its busy open market. The narrow streets were crowded with street merchants. Dealers, camel traders, and nomads all came to Parthos to buy and trade goods. On one corner, a merchant sold mesquite pods, a native desert food that could be ground into a hearty flour. Another sold prepared cactus leaves, sliced and ready to be cooked. Even more sold camel milk and yogurt, which was always abundant and nutritious. Fermented camel's milk (called *shubat*) was sold all over the city.

There were also a few outsiders—ebony-skinned nomads selling their wares before heading out to the desert again in the evening. They sold bone knives, saddles, dried goods, and beaded leather clothing. Their women sold intricate baskets, hand-woven so tightly that they could hold water.

The city was alert, but at peace. And overhead, observing everything, flew a dragon rider.

It was Sela and her carnelian dragon, Brinsop. The dragon's rust-colored scales glittered in the blistering sun. Sela's dragon was full-grown, and as a carnelian dragon, she was the smallest of the species. But she was still an impressive sight. When standing on her hind legs, Brinsop was over fifteen feet tall and weighed more than the largest horse. Her scales matched the color of the gem at her throat. Sela wore the gem's counterpart proudly on her neck, hung from a thick silver chain. It was the only jewelry she wore.

Sela, how are you holding up? We've been out here for hours already, and it seems hotter than normal today.

Brinsop communicated with Sela using the dragon stone. To an observer, a dragon's speech sounded like grunts and snorts, but Sela understood it perfectly.

"Perhaps we should go back. I'm getting uncomfortable in this heat, and my waterskin is empty. Let's return to the castle, rest for a moment, and eat."

Brinsop turned, flapping her wings in the stagnant air. She circled and landed on the castle ramparts. There were two other dragons there. They were Orshek and Karela, the orphaned clutchmates. They sunned themselves lazily, rubbing their black hides ecstatically on the warm earth. Their mother and other siblings had been killed by dragon hunters only a few months ago. Orshek and Karela survived because they had hatched weeks early.

The hatchlings had been exploring inside their birthing cave when the dragon hunters descended on their family. Orshek and Karela could hear their mother shrieking with fear and agony, and as they rushed back to the nest, their mother sent them a desperate telepathic message. *Stop! Stay hidden! Stay silent! Do not show yourselves! Stay hidden! Stay silent!*

The siblings huddled together in terror, hiding while the dragon hunters slaughtered their mother and the rest of the hatchlings. When the dragon hunters searched the rest of the cave, the hatchlings concealed themselves. They escaped detection, but were too afraid to leave the cave. Instead, they struggled in the darkness for weeks, hunting mice and eating insects. They could smell the rotting bodies of their mother and siblings. At one point, they heard vultures and other scavengers fighting over the carcasses.

Weeks passed. Orshek and Karela existed in darkness. Sela and Brinsop found them by chance while exploring the outskirts of the Death Sands. The hatchlings were so emaciated and skittish that Sela had to cast a slumbering spell upon them and drag them out of the cave by their feet. Brinsop carried them back to Parthos one at a time.

In Parthos, they were treated and rehabilitated. The black dragons were considered juveniles now, but their bodies were underdeveloped. Onyx dragons are traditionally one of the largest dragon species, usually growing larger than a house. But after weeks of malnutrition and lack of sunlight, the hatchlings' growth was stunted. Eventually, they would mature enough to bear the weight of a rider, but they would never develop to the size of a normal black dragon.

Orshek and Karela became attached to Brinsop, the dragon who saved them. In time, they even started calling her "mother." Even now, they played on the castle roof because they preferred to keep Brinsop within their sights.

Look at you two, growled Brinsop affectionately. *Playing like baby hatchlings while the rest of us labor in the heat!*

But mother, we await your return, said Orshek. *Remember—you promised to take us hunting for wild ostrich.*

Orshek, I never promised to take you hunting. I told you and your sister to go—by yourselves. I want both of you to go out and practice hunting. You know that I can't go with you; I have my duties here with Sela. Stop squandering away your time. You don't have to go far, but do try to catch something larger than a rabbit for a change.

Why won't you come with us? pouted Karela, who was the shyer one. She, more than her brother, bore the emotional wounds of their isolation. When Brinsop went away on a scouting mission for a few days, Karela refused to eat.

When I was a hatchling, dragons half your age were already hunting on their own! said Brinsop, exasperated.

"Karela, please understand, we can't leave the castle when we're on watch," responded Sela.

Sela communicated with Karela and Orshek using her dragon stone. The young dragons were too inexperienced to block Sela's communication. They were forced to listen to her. They both sulked, but didn't say anything else.

Sela and I are on duty for the next four days. Why don't you ask Charlight and Hanko if you can go with them? They're planning a hunt this evening, suggested Brinsop.

Brinsop tried to encourage the adolescent dragons to explore the countryside, make friends with the other dragons, and enjoy hunting prey, but it was difficult. They were still dependent on Brinsop and Sela for everything.

We don't want to go with Charlight and Hanko. They're so bossy! said Orshek.

Brinsop swatted the two with her tail. *Stop complaining and go do something useful! Don't just lie here terrorizing the guards!*

Brinsop snorted smoke and rose up on her hind legs, demonstrating that she was serious. The little dragons frowned and scuttled away. They looked back a few times, trying to stoke some pity. Brinsop held her gaze steadily, and pointed out towards the desert. Once the young dragons reached the end of the wall, they took flight, exploring the desert by themselves.

Finally! snorted Brinsop. *Those two grow more stubborn every day.*

"They won't go far."

I know. But it's a start.

"They're obstinate because you spoil them. One minute you bellow at them, and the next minute you coddle them," said Sela.

Brinsop sniffed, but she did not argue. *I worry about them. They're not growing normally. Karela is so fragile, and Orshek is overprotective of his sister. They're fearful. There are so many unresolved issues. If they can't overcome them, they will never be able to take a rider, or even defend themselves properly.*

Sela patted Brinsop's side. "They're alive. Let us be thankful for that. They may be the only two black dragons left in the kingdom. We're lucky to have them."

Don't misunderstand me—I am thankful. I just wish we could do more. There are so few of us, and the ones who survive are all... impaired in some way. The emperor has decimated my kin. How many survive in the wild? A dozen? Maybe less? There are fewer mating females every year.

"I know it's discouraging, Brinsop. But we must continue to fight. We'll save as many as we can." Sela talked soothingly to her dragon. Then her stomach growled.

You're hungry; let's stop this depressing talk and eat. We've dawdled long enough.

Brinsop grabbed a few live chickens and swallowed them whole. The king kept live chickens on the fortress walls mainly to feed the dragons. They were cheap to raise and also laid eggs, so it was a good tradeoff. Sela found two eggs hidden in a crevice and cracked them onto a flat stone. Solar cooking was easy in the desert, and it saved precious fuel. The eggs bubbled up and cooked quickly. She scraped the steaming eggs off the stone with a knife and ate them. Then she filled her waterskin at the spigot and rested in the shade for a few minutes.

Just then, King Mitca walked up to the roof. Sela and Brinsop gave slight bows. Before the war, dragon riders bowed to no one, not even the emperor. But now most dragons and their riders bowed to King Mitca as a sign of fealty and respect. His kingdom was the last refuge for dragons and their riders—the only place they could live in relative safety. More than anyone else, he was responsible for the dragons' survival. Without Mitca, it was likely that every dragon would have been killed by the emperor.

"Sela, Brinsop." He nodded, acknowledging their gesture of respect. "I have news that I must share with all the riders privately. Call the others back to the city. This is important for everyone to hear."

"Yes, my lord," Sela responded. She closed her eyes and touched Brinsop to augment her power. Telepathic communication was not one of her strengths, especially at long distances. She focused, reaching out with her mind to all the dragons in the realm. There were six dragons in Parthos, only four of which had riders. Sela and Brinsop had been bound together the longest.

Charlight and Hanko were next. Charlight was also a carnelian dragon—a female. Hanko was a human rider.

Then there was Duskeye and Tallin, the wild pair. Duskeye was a male sapphire dragon, and his rider, Tallin, was a rare dwarf half-ling—half dwarf and half human. The youngest rider was an elf half-ling—a female named Riona. Her male dragon was called Stormshard. Stormshard was also a carnelian dragon.

Sela instinctively grasped the dragon stone around her neck. Her mind reached out; tendrils of thought streaked across the desert. She stood, trance-like, while searching for the minds of the others. It was always difficult to find the other riders, mainly because their minds were so guarded. They had learned to protect themselves from magical attacks. Sela found Riona and Stormshard first, sparring on one of the rocky outcroppings near the city.

"Riona, Stormshard—please return to the castle. The king has called us all back for an urgent meeting. Do you know where the others are?"

Sela's neck veins bulged under the strain. Although she had decades of magical training, she could only communicate telepathically with difficulty. The farther the distance, the greater the exertion. Even with Brinsop's considerable assistance, it was a struggle for her.

"We hear and obey, Mistress," said Riona. "Charlight and Hanko are in the north, searching for wild dragons. Duskeye and Tallin flew south, hunting ostrich with the black fledglings. We saw them pass some time ago; they invited us to hunt with them."

"Please contact them and tell them to return to the city at once."

"As you command, Mistress."

Riona and Stormshard broke contact abruptly. It was jarring, but Sela and Brinsop were used to it. Riona and Stormshard were both young and inexperienced, but Riona was a powerful telepath. Contacting the other dragon riders would be easy for her. Eventually, Riona could become the most powerful of all the dragon riders in Parthos.

Sela exhaled and sat down for a moment to gather her strength. "Whew!" Her head was pounding from the effort.

"Did you find them all?" asked the king.

"Yes. They're all nearby. Riona will call the rest of them back. They'll all be here within the hour."

"Excellent. Come with me. We have much to discuss."

"What about the aerial watch?" asked Sela.

"I will double the palace guards in the towers and put everyone on high alert. This news cannot wait. I need to pick up a scroll in my private quarters, and then I will meet all of you in the fortress cathedral." The king turned and walked briskly down the stairs.

I wonder what this is all about, said Brinsop.

"Your guess is as good as mine. Maybe the scouts found something interesting." Sela mounted Brinsop for the short flight to the cathedral.

It's been months since King Mitca has called a meeting like this, so the news must be important. He's smart enough not to bother us with little particulars, said Brinsop.

The cathedral was on the lowest level of the city. It was dedicated to Golka, the goddess of war and defense. A statue of the black-skinned goddess stood at the entrance.

She had a flaming sword in each hand. Two of her eyes were in the front, but Golka also had an eye in the back, so that no one could ever attack her from behind.

The cathedral was usually filled with worshippers. It was one of the only places in the cramped city that was spacious enough for all the dragons and their riders. Mitca's guards had emptied the building and searched it hours before in preparation for the king and his riders. For this and other sensitive tasks, the king always used his private guard.

Sela and Brinsop arrived first and entered the church gates without opposition. Seven heavily armed guards stood at the entrance. They nodded to the rider and her dragon, but otherwise did not move. Sela marveled at these men. Their full-body tattoos identified them as members of the king's personal honor guard. The ornate tattoos were not merely for decoration; they were comprised of ancient symbols—protective inscriptions to ward off hexes, curses, and other evil spells.

Mitca's private sentinels were all descendants or relatives of Fivan, the soldier that had saved him as a child. Fivan guarded Mitca throughout his life, and even helped build and design the city of Parthos. The tale of Fivan's death was well-known throughout the city. Mitca never let anyone forget it.

Fivan insisted on sampling all of Mitca's food before the king would eat it in order to prevent a poisoning attempt. Mitca was impetuous and brash, and like any young man he thought Fivan was too cautious. Mitca playfully called him "mother hen"—even clucking when he came into the room.

But Fivan's caution was well-founded. He knew that Vosper's treachery was boundless. In the end, Fivan died protecting his master.

Starfruit was a rare treat; it perished quickly and had to be smuggled in from southern Durn. It was prohibitively expensive, and Mitca craved the fruit often. Fivan insisted on eating part of the starfruit.

"My king, you must wait. I will taste the starfruit first. Then you may eat the rest."

"Fivan, you're too cautious! I don't want to share this with you. I only get starfruit once a year and I want this all to myself."

"That is all the more reason for us to be vigilant. My lord, please agree, or I will be forced to throw the entire plate out the window." Fivan smiled, but Mitca could tell that he was serious.

Mitca sighed. "Fine! I don't know why I let you intimidate me. I am the king!"

Fivan laughed quietly and took a bite from the costly fruit. A few minutes later, he collapsed to the floor in convulsions. The starfruit had been laced with kudu oil, a powerful poison made from the kuduare plant. Kudu was called the "death berry" because ingesting a minute amount was enough to kill a grown man.

Mitca, impatient, had also eaten a piece of the fruit, but was able to vomit in time to save his own life. Even so, Mitca spent weeks between life and death. Healing mages attended his bedside day and night. Eventually, Mitca recovered, but the experience made him a changed man. The oil caused permanent damage to Mitca's esophagus, and he never ate starfruit again.

The king buried Fivan's body in an ornate tomb in the cathedral, and he mourned Fivan for a year. He never forgave himself for Fivan's death, and he vowed to treat Fivan's family as his own. Shortly after the funeral, Mitca took all of Fivan's children and his widow and moved them into a private wing in the castle. Fivan's nine sons became his private guard. It had been so ever since. The sons of Fivan are The Nine—his private guard.

"We have arrived," announced Riona as she appeared with Stormshard at the cathedral doors. "The others should be here in a few minutes."

Charlight and Hanko appeared next, and then Duskeye and Tallin a few minutes later.

"Where are the fledglings?" asked Charlight.

"We left them at the fortress. I told them to watch the gates. It gives them something to do and makes them feel useful," replied Tallin, his red curls bobbing as he spoke. Tallin was handsome, fine-featured, but short and stocky. A thick scar ran from his cheek down to his shoulder and disappeared below his tunic. Tallin's dragon, Duskeye, also bore evidence of grievous wounds, including a pronounced limp and a cloudy right eye, which was sightless. Neither one ever talked about the source of their injuries.

Tallin never spoke of his upbringing or his childhood. The others only knew that he had been born in Mount Velik, along with other dwarves. Once Tallin discovered his magical gift, his life changed. He was spirited away from Mount Velik to Aonach Tower, where he thrived under the tutelage of the Masters.

When Duskeye accepted him as a rider, Tallin was overjoyed. Rider and dragon were inseparable. Tallin and Duskeye ate together, slept together, hunted together. They survived the emperor's butchery because of their fierce bond. When the emperor started hunting dragons, Duskeye and Tallin left for the desert and lived in hiding for decades.

Sela eventually found them by chance. Tallin almost killed Sela out of panic at being discovered. Sela and Brinsop tried to convince them to come out of hiding, but it still took many months of careful persuading for them to agree to come to Parthos. Even now, they refused to remain within the city's walls for any extended period, preferring to live in the desert.

"All of you are here—good." Mitca walked into the cathedral. As usual, all of the dragons and their riders offered slight bows to the king, except for Tallin and Duskeye. They never bowed to anyone.

"Everyone, I have news from the east." Mitca pulled a scroll from his waistband and unrolled it. "I received an urgent message from one of my informants last night. An emerald dragon stone has been found in Darkmouth Forest. This scroll bears a rubbing of the engraving. It is a rider's stone—I suspect the stone was Chua's."

"Chua? That's impossible," said Sela. "Chua and his dragon, Starclaw, were killed years ago. They fell from the sky during the Great War. I saw it with my own eyes."

"I know it sounds implausible, but who else could it belong to?" replied Mitca. "It is a rider's emerald. Green dragons are rare, almost as rare as white dragons. But if the dragon stone is intact, then it is likely one of them is still alive. Perhaps both of them are."

Charlight shook her great head. *Chua cannot still be alive. It would be insanity for him to remain near the capital city. Even if he was alive, the dragon hunters would have found him by now. And even if the hunters couldn't find him, the emperor's necromancers would have.*

Sela communicated Charlight's comment to the king, while nodding in agreement. "I agree with Charlight. The stone must be a forgery."

Tallin cleared his throat and then spoke quietly. "A forgery is unlikely. Mitca is right. If the dragon stone is intact, then they are probably alive. Chua may be in stasis, and Starclaw may be in hibernation. It is possible to stay alive in this way and expend very little energy. It even helps repair injuries. Duskeye and I know from experience."

Duskeye dropped his snout and touched Tallin. *If both of them had died, the stone would have splintered. A strong cloaking spell could have concealed them, even in the east.*

"This is foolishness. Who has the power to maintain a cloaking spell for that long? It's impossible!" scoffed Riona.

"We can," replied Tallin. "Duskeye and I learned how to sustain our cloaking spells for months at a time."

"B-but that's impossible! Cloaking spells are exhausting—how can you possibly endure the strain for so long? Even while you sleep?" Riona sputtered.

Tallin turned to Riona with steely eyes and said, "To underestimate our powers would be a mistake, *elf*. Do not forget that I have dwarvish blood. I am much stronger than I look. The more one practices the magical arts, the stronger one becomes. Duskeye and I concentrated our studies on concealment spells. There is not a mage in the kingdom who could find us if I did not want them to."

"Let's get back on track, everyone," Sela said. "I do not believe that Chua and Starclaw are alive. How could they be—after all these years? Isn't it more likely that the stone is a forgery?"

"It is real," answered the king. "My informant is a mage. Her powers are marginal, but she could still feel the stone's energy. She tested it herself."

"Can your mage be trusted?" asked Hanko.

"Yes. She is beyond reproach. She fought in the Orc Wars, and her husband was a rider. He was killed by the emperor during the war."

"Her husband was a rider? What was his name?" asked Riona, her almond-shaped eyes wide with surprise.

King Mitca's eyes narrowed. "I would... rather not say."

Riona bit her lip, her face burning with embarrassment. Some secrets were too precious to repeat. She knew the king could not risk revealing the identity of his informant, even to the dragon riders. Spies were everywhere, and the emperor was ruthless. Some minor detail, whispered in passing, could seal all their fates.

Mitca passed the scroll to Sela. It appeared to be blank. There was a glamour on the scroll—not strong enough to deter anyone with magical abilities, but enough to prevent a normal human from reading the text.

Sela recited a simple incantation and runes appeared. She narrated the letter. "It says—'*Your Royal Highness, I must inform you that a dragon stone has been found in the east. It is in my possession. I tested it with spells and I can say with certainty that it is real. I will keep it hidden as long as I can. Please send orders. Faithfully yours.*' That is all. It is signed with a symbol instead of a name." Sela passed the scroll around to the others.

"All of our informants sign with a symbol, and they only send messages in the old language. It makes communications safer," said the king.

The writing was rudimentary—everyone could tell that the writer had not studied the old language for very long. However, the image of the dragon stone was crystal clear. The stone had been placed underneath the parchment, and charcoal had been rubbed over the image, creating an impression. The carving depicted a dragon's head, breathing fire.

When the scroll passed to Duskeye, he examined it and frowned.

"If the stone is not a forgery, then it is Chua's," said Tallin. "I recognize it."

"Are you sure?" asked Riona. "There were hundreds of dragon riders before the war broke out."

Tallin responded to Riona flatly, "I'm sure."

Mitca said, "It is too dangerous for me outside the Death Sands. I pass this information to you so you may decide what you want to do. I cannot leave. I will offer asylum to Chua and Starclaw, if you can get them back to Parthos alive. That is the best I can do." King Mitca took the scroll and tucked it back in his waistband. "If you decide to search for them, then let me know and I will send word to the informant. She will put the stone in a safe place where you can retrieve it."

The king turned to go. "I will leave four of my guards at the cathedral doors to ensure your privacy. When you exit, dismiss them, and they will return to the castle. You have one day to decide what you want to do."

"And what if we cannot come to a consensus?" asked Sela.

"If you cannot come to an agreement, I will order my mage to destroy the stone. I cannot risk it falling into enemy hands," the king said as he left the cathedral. "I leave you to decide."

The king walked out into the street, and his private guard surrounded him. A few guards stayed behind as promised. One popped his head inside the cathedral and addressed the group.

"The king has ordered us to escort Mistress Sela and her dragon back to his private quarters after your meeting is adjourned." Then he turned back and sealed the door. It closed with a thump.

"A dragon stone can't be destroyed—can it?" asked Riona.

"Yes... it can," answered Sela. "But only with difficulty. The stone can't be destroyed when it's in the rider's possession, except by killing the rider. However, when a stone is separated from its rider, it can be shattered using necromancy. During the war, the emperor's necromancers would try to kidnap a dragon or a rider, remove the dragon stone, and destroy it using dark magic. The magical shockwave would usually kill the rider and the dragon, so it was like killing two birds with one stone. More often than not, the spell would kill the necromancer as well. It's an evil thing to shatter a dragon stone."

Sela sat down and sighed. "So, what are we going to do?"

If Starclaw is alive, we must find her. We can't leave her to die in the east, said Charlight.

"It's too dangerous," said Riona. "There aren't enough of us. We can't risk one to save another. It could be a trap."

"How about the rider? Is it possible that Chua is still alive?" asked Sela.

"It's doubtful. And even if he was alive, none of us should risk our lives to save him," spat Hanko.

"Why not? Isn't saving the rider just as important as saving his dragon?" said Riona.

"Chua was a traitor, Riona," replied Hanko.

Riona gasped with surprise. "A dragon rider who was a traitor? I never knew this—how come the others don't talk about it?"

"Now, now, everyone… let's not jump to conclusions," said Sela. "No one is sure what happened. Chua disappeared during the war, after falling from the sky in battle. Most assumed that he and Starclaw were dead, but there was some spotty evidence that both had defected to the other side and had been working as double agents for the empire, as spies."

Hanko spoke again, "Chua was an oathbreaker! Hundreds of dragons and their riders may have perished because of him."

Hanko, no one knows for sure. There is one other possibility, said Duskeye quietly.

"What else could it be?" asked Sela. "The stone exists, so Chua and Starclaw must both still be alive."

Starclaw could be waiting in Darkmouth Forest for her new rider to mature, replied Duskeye. *Chua was gravely injured during the war. Of that, I'm certain. But Chua was still alive when he fell from the sky. What if Chua had a child? If a magical transfer was done, then the child would be able to take the original rider's place.*

Hanko scoffed, "Unlikely! How could a dragon stay hidden for so long in the east? And how could they have made a transfer without anyone discovering it? This is foolishness!"

"No. I disagree. It's possible, and in fact it makes perfect sense. It explains why Chua and Starclaw disappeared," said Tallin. "Chua had a lover during the war. I saw them together at least once or twice. A peasant woman. The woman was with child. Even if gravely injured, Chua could have done a transfer, even if the child was an infant. I've seen it done... in desperation... at least once before."

Sela sighed. "I have serious reservations about this. It may be a trick. But we cannot ignore it. The only thing left to decide is... who is going to leave the safety of the Death Sands to look for Starclaw, and possibly Chua?"

No one spoke. Then Duskeye said, *Tallin and I will volunteer.*

Everyone looked at the pair in surprise. Tallin and Duskeye never volunteered for anything.

"Duskeye, are you *sure*?" asked Sela.

"Yes. We'll go," Tallin responded. "Duskeye and I understand something of how Starclaw must be feeling. I, too, was separated from Duskeye for an extended period— to be alone, for so long... after bonding to a dragon, it is... unbearable."

Sela and Riona shivered involuntarily.

Tallin is the strongest illusionist, and he will conceal us with ease. It would be riskier for anyone else to go, said Duskeye.

"You have a point," nodded Sela. "But where will you go first? Darkmouth Forest is vast."

"I have an instinct, and I will follow it," said Tallin. The others waited for him to elaborate, but he did not offer anything more. Duskeye nudged his rider, but also remained silent. Their thoughts were guarded, as always.

"You've made an honorable choice. I'll report our decision to the king," said Sela.

"It is decided then. Duskeye and I leave for Darkmouth Forest tonight," said Tallin.

The Mage's Flame

Elias awoke with a start. It had been exactly one week since he found the dragon stone. His dreams had grown more disturbing. When he closed his eyes at night, he dreamt only of dragons. When he woke up, his mind wandered and he daydreamed of dragons. He rubbed his eyes and peeked outside the window. It was snowing. Again.

His grandmother was already awake, stirring porridge in the kitchen.

"Good morning, Elias. I'm using some of your honey to make breakfast. I got fresh goat's milk this morning from Borgil. He still owed me for sewing up his arm two months ago." She put the wooden spoon to her lips and tasted, nodding with satisfaction. "It's only wheat gruel, but it's sweet and delicious."

Elias got up and put on his cloak. "It's freezing. A hot breakfast sounds wonderful." He walked over and inhaled the aroma of bubbling porridge.

"It snowed last night, and it will continue to snow throughout the week," Carina said. "These mountains are colder than the valley. It's a trade-off. We're safer from bandits and the emperor's tax collectors, but we have to deal with more severe weather. The mountains and the forest offer us protection."

"I still wish it was warmer." He shivered. "Grandmother, are the Death Sands hot all the time, even in the winter?"

"Yes. It's always warm in the Death Sands, although the temperatures are milder in the fall and winter. The desert is treacherous. A healthy man can die there in just a few hours. The Death Sands are filled with dangerous creatures, nomads, and bandits. One should never underestimate the power of the desert."

"Have you ever been to the Death Sands, Grandmother?"

"Yes, many years ago, before you were born. I dare not speak of it much; it is a rebel territory, after all. It's best to keep quiet about such things." She looked wistfully at the ceiling. "It's beautiful, though. In all of Durn, there's no place like it. At night, you can see a million stars in the sky. There are no clouds. In the spring, the rain comes and the cactus flowers bloom purple and white. There's nothing as lovely as the desert in bloom. And there are the dragons. It's amazing to see them fly free."

"Tell me, what do they look like?" Elias started to ask her more questions about the desert, but was distracted by shouting outside.

"What was that?" asked Carina.

"I don't know." Elias peeked out the window. "There's something going on in the village. I see men on horses. They're dressed in yellow and red."

Carina rushed to the window, pulling away the sackcloth curtain. "Elias!" she gasped. "Those are empire soldiers! They're coming towards us!"

The men were still a good distance away, but their armor and horses set them apart. These were the emperor's men.

Elias ran to the door, but Carina shoved him back. She grabbed his shoulders and twisted him around to face her. Her knuckles were white.

"Elias—tell me the truth—did you tell anyone else about the stone?" Carina whispered anxiously.

"I—y-yes. I tried to sell it to Frogar a few days ago. I-I'm sorry! I thought I could get some money—to help us through the winter!" His eyes filled with tears. He had never seen his grandmother this frantic.

"Don't cry—just tell me—where is the stone now?"

"It-it's in my room, hidden." Elias quivered. "I-I didn't take the stone back to the forest, like you asked me. I was going to take it to Jutland and sell it. I'm sorry! I'm so sorry!"

"Stop crying—and listen to me carefully. It's too late to do anything about it now. We don't have much time. These soldiers will kill me, Elias."

"What? No—no! Don't say that!" Elias began to sob.

"Stop! Be strong! You must escape with the stone. Go to Darkmouth Forest. Follow the path to the Elder Willow." Carina rushed to the cabinet and pulled out a little dagger and a worn journal. "Use the map in this book. The Elder Willow is well-hidden, so you must continue to look for it until you find it. Take this dagger; it's enchanted. No one will be able to take it from you without your permission. Guard this book—it's my grimoire. All my knowledge of spells is in here; safeguard it well."

"Grandmother—please!" Elias' chin trembled. "You're scaring me!"

"Elias—I'm sorry I can't explain, but nothing can be done about it now. Go to your room, swiftly! Get Grandfather's cloak and your knapsack."

Elias ran to his room, pulling on his boots. He donned his warmest cloak and ran back out to the kitchen.

"Grandmother?" Hot tears ran down his cheeks. Elias was afraid.

Bang! Bang! The men pounded on the door. "Woman! Open the door. We're here upon orders from the emperor!"

"Be brave! Elias, here's some dried beef and your waterskin. Put them in your rucksack. Do you have the dragon stone?"

"Yes. It's here." Elias unclasped his fist, and it was there, shining in his palm.

"Hide it!"

Elias obeyed, tucking the stone into his boot.

Carina clasped his face in her hands. "I love you, my grandson. No matter what happens, remember that. Now go. Leave through the root cellar. Stay hidden until it's safe.

You'll know when. Then run to the forest and go straight to the Elder Willow! Don't look back, just keep running!"

Bang! Bang! "Open up! Or we'll break down the door!" the men yelled from outside, more forcefully this time.

"I'm coming! Hold on!" shouted Carina, and then whispering, "Elias—make haste! You must go!"

Carina lifted a worn rug in the kitchen, revealing a door. Elias slipped through the door in the floor and crawled down the rickety steps into the root cellar. He was underneath the cottage. Carina slammed the door shut. He heard his grandmother dragging the rug back over the opening. He tried to move, but fear kept him frozen in place.

His eyes adjusted to the faint light coming in from cracks. Above him, he heard the front door open and loud footsteps—the soldier's boots. He could see movement through a crack in the floor. Elias paused, listening closely.

"Old woman—we heard you found a stone in the forest—where is it? Tell us quickly, and I might let you live." It was a man's voice—gruff and angry.

"A stone?" Carina responded. "I don't know anything about it. If I had something so precious, I would have sold it and bought myself some food! The emperor isn't feeding me, after all." Her voice did not betray a hint of fear.

"You don't know anything about it, eh? How about your grandson? I want to talk to him. Where is he?" asked the soldier.

"I don't have a grandson. I live alone," said Carina.

"Do you take me for a fool, woman?" roared the man.

"Yes! You are a fool!" Carina screamed. "A wretched fool! Are you going to attack an old woman? Get out—get out of my house!"

Elias gasped, his hand going up to his mouth. He had never heard his grandmother talk like this. Elias heard a dull thump and a crash.

He heard a groan. It was his grandmother's voice. They had thrown her to the ground—an old woman! These men were beasts. Elias swallowed a lump in his throat, but he kept silent.

"Tell me where to find the boy—and the stone. Or I will kill you, woman. Now talk!"

Elias heard the sounds of other men stomping into the cottage. Some of them were laughing.

"It is true... I am an old woman." Carina spat blood. "I'm weak... I've been sick for a long time. But appearances can be deceiving. You've underestimated me, and that will be your doom."

The soldier chuckled. "Is that so?"

Two more soldiers stepped inside. They shut the door behind them, so the villagers couldn't see what they planned to do.

"Yes, it is so. I was simply waiting for all of you to arrive." Carina's hands glowed fire-red, and she jerked her fists in the air.

"By Golka! Captain, she's a mage!" one of the men shouted. "Stop her!"

The door hinges melted shut, trapping all the men inside.

"The door! It's sealed shut! She's cast a spell on it!" another cried.

"Kill her!"

The men descended on Carina, but it was too late. Her body had turned bluish-white. They touched her skin and their hands burned.

"Augghh! She's on fire!" the men screamed.

The heat inside the cottage increased, and the air began to crackle.

"Enjoy my hospitality, you fiends! *Incêndio!*" Carina roared, and the men burst into flames, screaming in agony. Their clothing, hair, and bodies burned in blue fire—the mage's flame. The spell took enormous reserves of energy, and Carina collapsed, taking her last breath. The cabin filled with acrid smoke, and it started to creep into the root cellar.

Smoke trickled into the cellar. Elias could no longer see anything. He stumbled and fell in the darkness, swearing as his knee hit the ground. The cellar was almost empty, but he knew there were some onions and turnips in the corner. He felt around in the darkness until he found the vegetables, and then added them to his pack. Holding back tears, he exited the cellar. *She sacrificed herself to save me.*

Fragrant black smoke filled the air; all of Carina's herbs were burning. Elias had cover to escape. He had to leave now—before the rest of the village discovered what was happening. As he reached the forest's edge, he could hear dogs howling and villagers shouting. Behind him, his neighbors screamed, "Fire! Fire!" Elias ran, without looking back.

Thorin Ulfarsson

Elias ran for many leagues without stopping, until he was far from the village. When his side ached, he continued to walk as fast as he could. The weather was miserable, and a slow drizzle of freezing rain began to fall. He walked deeper into the forest, staying off the paths.

I should have obeyed my grandmother the first time, he thought. He would return the stone to the tree where he found it. After that, he would travel to the Elder Willow, as his grandmother had ordered him. He tried to control his emotions, but as soon as he stopped to rest, his eyes filled with tears.

He shook his head, and tried to concentrate on escaping. Elias was grateful for his wool cloak, which kept him warm even when wet. He was also thankful for the weather because the rain would help hide his tracks.

He eventually reached the clearing where he had found the stone over a week ago. As he walked towards the tree, Elias was surprised to see a boy on the ground, face down. His curiosity overcame his fear, and Elias went to the boy's side, tapping his shoulder.

"Hey! Boy—are you all right?"

The figure spun around in a flash and grabbed his arm. Elias was shocked to see that it wasn't a boy, but a little man—a black-bearded dwarf, no more than four feet tall, his face wrinkled like an old potato. But none of his hair was streaked with gray. It was impossible to tell his age.

His eyes were like bits of black coal. "Who are ye?" he asked.

"I—I'm Elias! I'm here to... return something. I thought you were a boy."

He laughed. "I'm not a boy, I'm a dwarf! Haven't ye ever seen a dwarf before?"

Elias shook his head. "No—never. Are you hurt? Why are you lying on the ground like that?"

"I fell from the tree. I was tryin' to reach inside. Me old bones don't move like they used to. Dwarves don't belong in trees, I'll tell ye that much." He groaned and touched his forehead, which had a quickly rising bump. "Blast! I can't wait to be gone from this freezin', miserable forest and back to Mount Velik!"

He got up with some difficulty, and extended his hand. "The name's Thorin—Thorin Ulfarsson—what's yers, boy?"

"My name's Elias," he said cautiously. "What were you looking for? Can't you see there's a beehive in there?"

The bees were buzzing slowly in the air, still coming in and out of the hole in the tree.

Thorin's eyes lit up and he laughed. "I'm not afraid of bees, boy. A little bee sting isn't goin' to affect me much—there's precious little for them to go after!"

He had a point. The dwarf wore his long hair in a braid, and his beard was also pleated. Every patch of skin was covered with jet black hair—even his ears and knuckles. He was like a bear—only his nose, mouth, and tiny black eyes were exposed.

"So, you're Elias, eh? Why, ye're almost a full-grown man!" Thorin clapped him on the back so hard that Elias coughed.

"Yes... I had my fifteenth cycle. H-How do you know me?"

"I don't know *you*, boy. I knew your *grandmother*, Carina. She's the one who sent me the message, and I came as soon as I could. I'm glad ye're here. It saves me the trip all the way to Persil."

"Message? What message? My grandmother didn't tell me anything about you," said Elias with suspicion. Then he sighed. "But—she didn't tell me much of any-thing—she always had her secrets. Thorin...my grand-mother is dead. Soldiers came to our village this morning. They forced their way into the cottage and attacked her. She died trying to save me."

Elias sat down, putting his head in his hands. He started sobbing.

"Ah, I'm sorry, lad. That's a shame. Carina was a fine woman." Thorin patted Elias' shoulder. "Yer grandmother died an honorable death. She was a friend of my people. She was fearless, too—one day I will tell ye some stories. But there's no time for sorrows. Do ye have the dragon stone with ye?"

"Y-Yes," admitted Elias. "I was trying to put it back where I found it. My grandmother told me to return it days ago, but I disobeyed her. I tried to sell the stone last week. The man I tried to sell it to—he's a bad man. I'm certain that's how the soldiers found out about it." Elias' voice cracked. "It's my fault she's dead."

"Now, now, there's no reason to be blamin' yerself, lad. Ye couldn't have known."

"I'm just trying to be rid of it—the stone has been bad luck since I found it."

Elias pulled the stone out of his pocket and showed him. Thorin's eyebrows went up, but he did not touch the stone.

"Aye, that's a true dragon stone. Yer grandmother asked me to come and get it—take it back to Mount Velik for safekeepin'. The plan was for me to take the stone back to our vaults. But I'm guessin' our plans have changed."

"I don't know what to do. I've never traveled outside Darkmouth Forest."

"Well, it looks like we'll be traveling companions then," said Thorin.

"Okay." Elias looked visibly relieved. "I can't go back to the village… probably not ever."

"Yes, I'm sure ye're right. The reward for a dragon stone is tempting—the emperor offers a hundred gold crowns to anyone who brings him one. Times are bad, and neighbors can't be trusted when they're starvin'."

"A hundred crowns!" Elias gasped. It was a vast fortune. "I should have just taken the stone to the emperor!"

"No, boy. Be glad ye didn't. It's a fine bit o' coin, but the emperor would spit ye alive. Ye can't enjoy a reward if ye're rottin' in the ground!" Thorin examined the stone carefully in Elias' palm. "Yup. A true dragon stone that is. Hide it securely. We can't afford to lose it now."

Elias shook his head. "Can you tell me what's going on? I don't understand any of this."

"Don't worry, boy. I'll explain it to ye in due time. Are ye sure that yer grandmother killed *all* the soldiers?"

"Yes—I'm sure. The whole house went up in flames. No one escaped."

"Good. That means it's safe for us to make camp. It will be at least another four days until old Vosper can get more soldiers up to Persil, and we'll be long gone by then. Yer granny was always thorough, I'll tell ye that! What a woman! May her spirit live forever in the fields of' Darthnell, enjoyin' all the spoils of the afterlife."

Thorin made a circular motion on his chest and withdrew a gold amulet from around his neck. It was a pendant, set with tiny rubies, and it bore the image of a claw hammer. He kissed it before tucking it back into his tunic.

"What is that?" asked Elias, pointing to the pendant.

Thorin held it up proudly. "This is the symbol of me clan, *Marretaela*. My people are honest folk, though not the biggest clan. We can talk more about this later. Right now, let's go make camp. There's a secluded cave a few miles north o' here. We shouldn't stay out in the open—there's no sense in taking unnecessary risks. The sun will be goin' down soon, and we could have a fire started before then. It will be freezin' tonight and we'll need to stay warm. Plus, I'm not one for cold food. I caught a rabbit earlier that we can enjoy for dinner tonight."

Elias nodded. "There are good mushroom beds nearby. It will only take me a few minutes to gather some. They'll go well with the rabbit."

"Aye. I'll help ye, boy." They walked to Elias' favorite mushroom spot and collected handfuls of wild mushrooms, which Thorin wrapped into a piece of cloth and tied to his belt.

"Let's go now, before it gets much later. My mount, Duster, is grazin' nearby. I'll go get him." Thorin returned a few minutes later with a sturdy gray pony. Elias reached out and patted his neck, and the animal responded by nudging him gently.

"He seems good-natured."

"Aye. Duster has been my favorite for years. He wasn't bred for speed—he was bred for endurance. He's as sharp as a tack and doesn't tire easily. The dwarves breed the best ponies and sheep in all of Durn. Our animals have vigor and fortitude, just like us!"

Thorin slapped the pony's side proudly. Duster responded with a loud whinny. The pony's legs were shorter than normal, and thick; they were knotted with muscle.

"Do ye know how to ride, lad?"

"Yes," answered Elias. "We owned a horse a few years ago, but Carina sold him because we needed money. I learned how to ride bareback; we couldn't afford a saddle."

"That's fine. Tomorrow, we'll head for Jutland. We'll purchase a horse for ye there."

"Thorin, my grandmother told me that I should go to the Elder Willow. Do you know where it is?" asked Elias.

"Yes. I suspected she might have told ye to go there."

"Do you know why?"

"Not really sure," Thorin said, looking at the ground. He cleared his throat. "The Elder Willow is a magical tree, and the groves surrounding the willow are guarded by various spells and tree sprites. It's not an easy journey, and the grove is considered a holy place. If Carina told ye to go, then we should try to go. The Elder Willow is a bit out of our way, so we'll travel to Jutland first."

"Okay… I just wish I understood what was going on."

"Everything will make sense in time. In the meantime, ye should collect some kindlin' for our fire. Gather as much as ye can. It will be cold tonight."

They were going to Jutland! Elias was excited. Jutland was the largest city in the Elburgian Mountains. He heard the village merchants talking about it often. There was a large marketplace and many wonderful sights. Elias' grandmother used to trade there before her health failed. Elias had only been there once—and that was many years ago when he was a child. He still remembered many of the sights and sounds.

Both started walking east, with Thorin leading the way. Elias kept himself busy collecting kindling for the fire. The dwarf hummed an old war song, but otherwise didn't say much.

After a short while, they reached the cave. Elias would have missed it if Thorin hadn't pointed it out. The cave entrance was covered by shrubbery.

"Here it is," said Thorin. "I camped here last night. It's a wee openin'—you'll have to crawl in—but it's larger inside. It's a good spot, and warm. We're far from the path and concealed from the wind. We'll sleep comfortably enough. Ye must get a good night's sleep because we'll be up before dawn. I'm goin' to get Duster settled, and I'll be back."

Elias crouched down and crawled into the opening. Once he got inside, he was pleased to see that the cave was large enough for him to stand, and it was roomy enough for two to sleep. Elias started to build a fire, laying the kindling in a little pile by the cave entrance. "*Incêndio!*" he said quietly, and the kindling caught fire. Thorin came back just in time to catch Elias using the spell.

"Usin' magic, eh?" said Thorin, as he poked his head into the cave opening. "Ye should learn how to build a fire properly, without magic. Magic is just a crutch."

"You startled me. My grandmother used to say that, too. She was a healer, but she rarely healed her own cuts and bruises. She said it was good for the body to heal itself; otherwise, it might forget how to do it."

"Yer grandmother was a wise woman."

"Grandmother always told me to keep my powers hidden. I *do* know how to build a fire without magic. I use magic because it's faster. Usually I hide it, but.... well... don't dwarves use magic, too?"

"Aye. We have our own spellcasters, although the mageborn gift is rare in our people. They're healers, mostly, but we also have some metalsmiths that can forge magical weaponry. Our enchanted blades are unmatched. Even more powerful than elvish swords." Thorin grabbed his pipe and stuffed it with smokeleaf.

Elias remembered the dagger that his grandmother had given him, and he pulled it out of his waistband. "My grandmother gave me this. I've never seen another one like it. Did the dwarves make it?"

Thorin examined the little dagger carefully. "Aye. This is a dwarvish blade. It's enchanted, too. It's a rare thing to see a human with a blade like this. I know the story behind it. Would ye like to hear it?"

"Yes! My grandmother hardly ever talked about her past."

"All right, but first help me with dinner. Then I'll tell ye all about it. I'll find some branches to make a spit for the rabbit."

"Okay, I'll cut the mushrooms and dress the rabbit for cooking."

Elias chopped the mushrooms, skewered them, and placed them on hot coals to cook. He gutted and cleaned the rabbit, burying the entrails outside, far away from the cave entrance. He didn't want to encourage any night-time scavengers. Thorin came back with some sturdy branches and lashed together a simple spit to cook the rabbit. A few minutes later, everything was sizzling over the fire, and Elias settled down to listen.

"Now yer grandmother was a fiery one! She spent time in Mount Velik durin' the Orc Wars. That was many years ago. She was one of the best healers we had—she saved many lives, human and dwarves alike. During one battle, I took a crushin' blow to my left shoulder. Although my chainmail saved me, many bones were broken underneath. Carina set the bones and healed me; I was back in the fight the next day. She had a true gift, that one."

"My grandmother fought in the Orc Wars?" asked Elias, incredulous.

"Yes, and the Dragon Wars, too. She fought the empire for most of her life." Thorin sat back and puffed his pipe wistfully. "What a woman! It's a shame she's gone, lad. I'm truly sorry for yer loss."

"Thank you," said Elias. He was genuinely surprised that Thorin knew so much about his grandmother. It seemed as if Thorin was talking about a stranger. "What about the story of the dagger?"

"Ah, yes. Well, as I said, yer grandmother was highly regarded by our people. Durin' the Dragon Wars, the emperor accused the dwarves of harborin' fugitive dragon riders. It wasn't true, but it was an excuse to attack us. My people fought back, withdrawin' into Mount Velik. Vosper tried repeatedly to overtake the mountain, but he never succeeded. Eventually we prevailed, but we lost many good men. Durin' the war, yer grandmother saved the life of Dracan Lindisfarne, who was the only son of Hergung Lindisfarne, a clan king. Hergung honored her, and she was given this dagger as a gift. Hergung went on to become the leader of all the dwarf clans."

Thorin flipped the blade in the palm. "This knife never needs sharpenin', and it can never be forcibly taken from ye, except by someone who shares yer bloodline."

"But Thorin, I handed the blade to you and nothing happened."

"Yes, but I'm not going to steal it!" said Thorin, wagging his finger at the boy. "The blade knows."

"But how?" asked Elias.

"Magic, my boy. How else? Treasure it. It may save yer life someday." Thorin handed the blade back to Elias.

"I wish I understood what was going on. I haven't had time to think—when I ran from the village, it was like a dream. I've never seen my grandmother do anything but healing spells. But today, she killed all those soldiers! I heard her yelling—but not in fear. She mocked them even! Then I heard explosions and smelled smoke."

"Yer grandmother was gifted with healing spells, but she picked up other spells here and there. One of our dwarf mages, Arik, was infatuated with her and taught her many incantations." Thorin's voice dropped and he cupped his hand to Elias' ear in an embarrassed whisper. "It's unseemly for dwarves and humans to carry on like that, but everyone knew that Arik was madly in love with yer grandmother. Nothin' ever came of it, though—she wouldn't have him, either because he was a dwarf, or because she was already in love with yer grandfather."

"You knew my grandfather? I never met him. He died before I was born."

"Yes, I met him, but only briefly. He was one of the other healers, a human mage like yer grandmother. He died durin' the war. By then, yer grandmother was already pregnant with yer mother." At that, Thorin grew quiet.

"My mother... I don't remember anything about her. Did you know her, too?" asked Elias.

"No... not really. After yer grandfather's death, Carina left Mount Velik. She was pregnant with yer mother, Ionela. I only met yer mother once—and only briefly. I don't remember much about her, I'm afraid." Thorin paused. "Yer grandmother suffered a great deal. First she lost her husband, then her daughter. I'm sure she sacrificed herself for you because she couldn't bear the possibility of losin' you, too."

Elias choked back tears. He decided to change the subject. "So... how did you know about the dragon stone?"

"Durin' the Dragon Wars, most of the riders went missing. The majority were executed, but some defected to the other side to fight with the emperor. These traitors were promised many things, includin' wealth and prestige. But in the end, they were all betrayed—after the war, the emperor killed all the dragons and their riders, even those who fought for him."

"Why does the emperor hate dragons so much?" asked Elias.

"It's not hate, lad. It's *fear*. Fear of the *prophesy*."

"What prophesy? How come I've never heard of it?"

"Because the emperor doesn't want you to know. Each race on Durn has its own books of revelation," explained Thorin. "Vosper burned most of them, but he can't access the dwarf libraries. In our book, the *Kynn Oracle*, it states that the emperor will eventually be slain by a white dragon and his rider. So the emperor has done everything to try and eliminate the threat. When he burned Aonach Tower years ago, the vast libraries of the mage guilds were lost. But we dwarves have our own libraries. Our history remains unbroken. The elves have their own libraries, too."

"So now only the dwarves and the elves know about the prophesy?"

"No. Many do—it's only that the emperor has tried to keep it a secret. Even the orcs have an oracle."

"The orcs? Really? I thought they were just mindless savages."

"Savages, yes. But mindless, no. Orcs have their own myths and history, although it is unwritten. They have an oral tradition instead. Their teachings are passed down through the alpha males of each tribe. It has been thus for thousands of years."

"How come I never learned any of this? And how do you know so much?"

"Boy—I'm a lot older than I look." Thorin winked. "As for learnin'—well, the emperor works hard to keep his citizens ignorant."

"Why is the emperor doing this? Why doesn't he just leave the dragons alone?"

"The emperor is mad, and power-hungry. Vosper's necromancers have learned how to extend his life and increase his powers. He's still mortal, but he's stopped aging. He's like a dwarf—he could live for hundreds of years. Vosper grows stronger with each passin' cycle."

"Did the dwarves fight against the emperor during the Dragon War?"

"Aye. We remained neutral for a time, choosin' to wait. But then Vosper attacked one of the dwarvish cities in the west, razing it to the ground. We joined the fight after that. Thousands of dwarves died durin' the war, and the emperor drove us all into Mount Velik. Forced to work together, all the dwarf clans fought side-by-side. He could not defeat all of us. The emperor was never able to take the mountain. In the end, it was a stalemate. We stayed in the mountain, and the emperor retreated back to his capital."

"Do all the dwarves live in Mount Velik?"

"Most of us do. Mount Velik is our last stronghold. There are some clans that have chosen to venture out again, and there's even a small dwarf outpost near the Death Sands. We do a fair amount of trade with King Mitca."

Elias fell silent. This information seemed unreal—dwarves, orcs, dragons—it was too much for his mind to digest. He wrapped his cloak tighter around himself, shivering as a gust of wind entered the cave. He wished he'd never found the dragon stone in the first place.

Thorin sat back, contentedly smoking his pipe. His hand touched his head again, feeling a bump that had risen when he fell from the tree. "Ouch," he winced. The spot was purple, like a robin's egg.

Elias reached out with a glowing finger and touched the spot on Thorin's forehead. "Stay still. I'll heal it for you." Elias closed his eyes, absorbed in the spell. "*Curatio!*" The bump started to shrink, and the bruise dissipated. A few minutes later, it was gone. The effort tired him, and Elias sunk to the ground, exhausted. It had been a very long day.

Thorin felt the spot, amazed to find the bump healed. "Nice job, boy. I'm much obliged." He smiled, "Ye've definitely got yer grandmother's gift."

"Thanks," smiled Elias. "I'm glad you're here, Thorin. Even if I can't tell what's going on."

"Everything will soon be clear, lad. Go to sleep. I'll take the first watch."

The fire was warm, and the sweet aroma of the smokeleaf was comforting. Elias was asleep within minutes.

Jutland

The next morning was freezing cold, but clear. Thorin awoke before dawn and boiled some chicory root, making a delicious hot beverage for both of them. "Here ye go, boy. Drink this up; it will warm yer bones." Thorin handed Elias half a cold biscuit and a steaming cup of root coffee.

"Thanks." Elias accepted the tin cup gratefully. "This smells wonderful."

"Yup, it's good for the stomach and the spirit. We have a long distance to cover. First we'll buy you a horse in Jutland. Then we'll travel to the Elder Willow."

"How long will it take for us to reach the Elder Willow?" asked Elias.

"On horseback? At least a fortnight. Maybe longer. It's at the eastern edge of the forest. We'll have to cross the Orvasse River, too."

"The Orvasse River! I've never traveled so far east."

"There's a first time for everythin', boy. After that, I expect that I'll be takin' ye back with me to Mount Velik, which is in the north, past the emperor's palace. We'll have to be very careful near Morholt."

"We're going to the capital?"

"No, we'll be goin' around it. I'm not sure if we'll be followin' the coast or travelin' inland. Either way, it's a dangerous journey. Get used to travelin', lad—ye're in for an adventure." Thorin smiled, but his eyes were serious.

They finished the rest of their breakfast in silence, and then Elias scattered the evidence of their fire and covered the coals with dirt. As they exited the cave, Elias noticed Duster grazing on a stubborn patch of grass. Thorin placed their packs on Duster's back, and they were off.

Both of them walked, with Duster trotting happily behind. Their pace was brisk. Elias warmed up quickly. After a few hours, he was so hot that he had to remove his cloak. They didn't stop for lunch—they ate cold rabbit and drank water along the way.

Thorin hummed old dwarvish songs most of the time. Elias understood a few words here and there— remnants of the old language that pervaded the speech of every race on the continent. Sometimes Thorin talked about the history of the dwarves and their accomplishments. It was interesting, if nothing else. Elias had never met another dwarf, and Thorin's stories seemed supernatural. From the stories, Elias deduced that Thorin was at least a hundred years old. He wanted to ask his age, but he wasn't sure if it was impolite to do so.

While he was growing up, Elias prodded his grandmother for information, and she was always reluctant to give it. Thorin spoke freely of his people and his grandmother's exploits. It seemed incredible that he was talking about the same person—Elias never imagined that his quiet grandmother had such a wild history.

The trees grew sparser as the afternoon wore on, and eventually they arrived at a clearing at the top of a hill. In the distance, Elias could see the city of Jutland on the horizon. The city appeared larger than he remembered.

"There she is, boy. Old Jutland. Looks pretty much the same as I remember. The walls are taller, and they've replaced the old wooden drawbridge for an iron gate. Everyone is more cautious, it seems. I'll put on me hood and ride Duster into the city. Although it's not unheard of for a dwarf to be travelin' this far south, it's best if we avoid attractin' any unnecessary attention."

Thorin mounted Duster and tucked his long beard inside his cloak. Riding on the pony, it was difficult to determine Thorin's height, and with his beard hidden away, he didn't look much different from anyone else coming into the city.

A few hours later, they arrived at the city gate and got in line behind a slew of merchants and peasants wandering into the city.

Thorin whispered, "Listen, boy, if anyone asks, my name's *Brand* and ye're my son, *Tyr*. We're here to buy a horse—no reason to lie about that. Keep yer story simple and ye're less likely to stumble on a lie. Keep your hood on—it will help conceal yer appearance and it won't seem odd because it's cold." Elias nodded.

They reached the city just after sunset. As they approached the gate, Elias became nervous. He couldn't help it. The hair on the back of his neck stood up. Two watchmen stood at the gate.

"What business do you have in Jutland?" asked the skinny guard, who had greasy hair and several missing teeth.

"We've come to Jutland to purchase a horse," answered Thorin.

The watchman eyed them both. He spotted Thorin's ornate iron brooch, and his eyes narrowed with suspicion. "Where are you coming from?" asked the watchman, this time with interest.

"We've traveled from Gardarsholm."

"Humph. That's a long way to travel for a horse. Why didn't ye just go to the city of Faerroe? It's a lot closer."

"There's a horse breeder I trust here—Everyone knows that Faerroe is full of cheats and thieves, and I don't want to buy an animal just to have it die on the way home!" spat Thorin. He pounded his fist into his palm for good measure.

"What's the name of your breeder friend?" asked the guard in one final attempt to trip him up.

"His name's Floki Revansson," replied Thorin calmly.

The guard was satisfied and waved them in. "Go ahead then. But stay out of trouble while you're here. I've got a funny feelin' about both of you!" The guard wagged his finger accusingly.

As soon as they were inside the city walls, Elias expelled a huge breath. "That was close!" he whispered.

"Aye. They're askin' a lot of questions. Everyone's on edge. There's somethin' afoot. We'd better get yer horse and leave as soon as possible. I'd hoped to spend at least a day in the city and partake of some ale and hearty food, but we shouldn't risk it. That's a shame because there are quite a few nice eateries in Jutland."

"So you've been here before?" asked Elias. "You knew the name of a horse breeder."

"Yes, I've visited Jutland a few times. Floki Revansson is me cousin. We were raised together. He's a half-ling—his mother was human and his father was a dwarf. He's a gifted breeder—he raises some of the best livestock outside of Mount Velik. My clan would gladly have him, but Floki prefers to live with humans."

They walked to the heart of the city. Beggars and cart merchants lined the streets. A toothless woman sold black bread from the back of a donkey cart, and another farmer sold bags of dried corn on the roadside. The streets were full of litter. Elias couldn't believe how dirty the city was.

"Don't they ever clean the streets?" asked Elias.

"The city square looks worse than I remember. Keep walking. Floki's house is in the north part of town."

They continued to walk north, and the neighborhood improved. The beggars disappeared. As the last of the light vanished, they found themselves before Floki's shop. A weathered sign hung from iron rings above. It said "Revansson" and displayed a carved image of a horse.

"This must be it," said Elias.

"Yes, I remember the sign. It's a good thing, too—all the other businesses have shut their doors for the night, and the streets are dark. I'm glad we found it." Thorin walked up to the door and pounded the knocker. "Ho, ho there! Open up!" He continued to bang on the door for several minutes.

"What the blazes? Come back tomorrow! We're closed!" The door flung open, and a short man greeted them with a scowl.

"What, you don't have time for an old friend?" Thorin removed his hood and winked.

A look of shocked recognition passed over Floki's face. "Thorin? Is that you?" he whispered.

"One in the same!" Thorin grabbed Floki in a rough embrace. "How are you, cousin?"

"What a surprise!" said Floki, with a wide grin. Then he whispered, "Let's chat inside. It's not safe to talk out in the open."

He ushered Thorin and Elias into the house, which was richly furnished and spotless. "I'll have my son put Duster in our stables for the night." Floki pointed a finger at his son, about eleven, and the boy jumped up immediately and grabbed Duster's reins.

"Yes, Father?" asked the boy.

"Parvel, make sure that the pony is fed. Don't dawdle. Come back inside as quickly as possible." The boy nodded and disappeared, leading Duster to the stable behind the house.

Thorin marveled at the boy. "This is Parvel? Amazin' how time flies. Last time I saw ye, he was just a babe."

"Yes, he's grown up fine and strong. We've recently had another child; this is my daughter, Molly." Floki pointed at a chubby brown-haired baby playing with a ragdoll in the middle of the floor. She giggled, revealing a single tooth. "My wife, Halda, is outside gathering firewood. She'll be back in a moment. Why don't you both sit down?"

Thorin and Elias walked into the cozy living room. It was tiny, but warm and inviting. "So... who's your friend?" asked Floki, nodding at Elias.

"This is Elias, grandson of Carina Dorgumir. We're traveling together, and Elias needs a mount. I'm hoping to buy one of your fine horses—at a good price, of course."

"Grandson of Carina, eh? I know something of your grandmother, boy. She's a legend," said Floki.

"A legend?" asked Elias, still surprised that so many people knew his grandmother.

"Yes. Your grandmother saved my father's life. She saved him more than once actually. Both of my parents died fighting in the Dragon War when I was seven. I was raised by Thorin's clan. We grew up as brothers."

"I'm sorry about your parents," said Elias. "Why did you leave Mount Velik?"

Thorin answered, "Even though my clan treated Floki like family, the other clans don't take kindly to halflings. They're discriminated against."

"Yes," nodded Floki. "I got tired of being treated like an outsider. I could always pass as human, so I left the mountain as soon as I was old enough to find a mate. I wandered the countryside for a bit, and I finally met Halda."

109

"So your wife is human?" asked Elias.

"My wife is one-quarter dwarf—she's a quarter-ling. Her grandmother was a dwarf. Once we found each other, we got married and settled in Jutland. I started breeding horses. Business is steady, so we've been here ever since."

A chubby blonde woman dressed in breeches and a long apron walked in through the back door, carrying a pile of cut firewood. She was a few inches taller than her husband, but otherwise they looked similar. Halda's hands were large and callused, proof of years of hard work.

"We have visitors this late in the evening?" she said. Then she saw Thorin and smiled broadly. "By the stars! Thorin, is that you? Why, you haven't aged a single day!" She hurried over and gave him a peck on the cheek.

"And you, my dear, are as pretty as the first day we met," smiled Thorin, winking.

"Oh stop, you old flirt!" Halda scolded playfully.

After introductions and a few pleasantries, Halda said, "You must be famished. I'll get you some hot stew and ale."

"That would be wonderful," said Elias. And he meant it.

"She's a good woman, that one," said Thorin, smiling at Floki and his family.

Floki's son returned from the stable and latched the door. Halda set the table with plenty of hot food and ale. They settled down to a hearty meal. Halda nursed the baby right at the table. The food was simple and delicious. Elias ate with relish.

After the meal, Halda ushered the children out of the living room to prepare them for bed. She closed the door, giving the men some privacy. Thorin gave Floki a brief account of their trip, but he didn't mention the dragon stone.

"Jutland seems changed, cousin," said Thorin.

Floki nodded gravely. "It's been worse the last few years, Thorin. There's more beggars and bandits than I've ever seen, and Jutland is crawling with empire soldiers. An army captain took one of my best stallions. He said it was 'for the empire'—but I didn't see any payment and probably never will! Halda and I've thought about moving, but where? Faerroe is even worse, and Gardarshlom already has three other horse breeders. It's certainly not safer anywhere else."

"Well, ye know ye'll always be welcome in my house, cousin."

"To be honest, we've even thought about traveling to Mount Velik. We'd have to sell everything in order to move. The house, the horses—we'd just keep a few for the journey. It's a terrible time to leave the city. Halda and Parvel can ride well, but Molly is still nursing. The road to Mount Velik is treacherous. It's no place for an infant." Floki shook his head with worry.

"Aye, ye're right. But I know somethin' that might help ye make a decision."

"What's that?" asked Floki, lifting his head from his hands.

"War is comin', my friend," said Thorin sadly. "Even as we speak, the emperor is massing his armies in the east. Our king, Hergung, already sent messengers to Parthos with a warnin'. The dwarves have remained neutral up 'til this point, but if Vosper attempts to march on Mount Velik, we'll join the fight."

"Is Vosper powerful enough to capture Mount Velik *and* Parthos?" asked Elias.

"Not yet... but he will be soon," replied Thorin. "Vosper instituted forced conscription in the capital. All able-bodied men in Morholt must join the army or die. They aren't given a choice. The emperor's necromancers bind the soldiers with magical oaths. If they try to defect, they're killed. Vosper is taking everyone above thirteen years of age. Already all the villages around the capital city have been emptied, leavin' only women, old men, and babies."

"Blast!" said Floki, pounding his fist on the table. "That means they'll take me and my son."

"Yes... most likely," said Thorin.

"And if we travel to Mount Velik?" asked Floki. "What can we expect there?"

"Ye'll likely be fighting for the dwarves. Either way, ye're stuck. Ye'll be forced to fight for one side or the other. There's no way around it really."

"What about the Death Sands? Do you think we could make it to Parthos?" asked Floki.

"Honestly? No," said Thorin. "It's a brutal trek, even without children. Ye'll have to get by Vosper's soldiers at the border, and then make yer way across the desert. Ye'll have a better chance reaching Mount Velik."

"You have given me much to think about." Floki sighed heavily. "I must speak with my wife, and we'll decide what to do together. Let's stop this discouraging talk. Now, how can I help you both?"

"I need a horse," said Elias. "We'll be traveling north to Mount Velik. It's too far to go on foot."

Elias glanced at Thorin. He left out the part about visiting the Elder Willow. He sensed it was something he shouldn't mention.

"All right. We'll choose a horse for you tomorrow. Tonight, both of you are my honored guests. Please make yourselves comfortable. The fire will keep you warm, but there are two wool blankets in the corner should you need them." Floki pointed near the fireplace, where two gray blankets were stacked neatly on top of a barrel.

"Thank you," said Elias. "This sure beats sleeping outside in the snow."

Floki retired to the bedroom. A few minutes later, Elias heard Floki talking to Halda in lowered voices. Moments later, he could hear Halda crying. The atmosphere was bleak, but Thorin seemed unfazed by it. He just kept humming softly as usual. He spread out a blanket on the floor and was snoring within minutes.

Elias couldn't sleep. He felt a whirlwind of emotions. Then he remembered his grandmother's journal—he'd almost forgotten about it. Elias crawled over to his pack and dug out the journal. He touched the leather gently, his eyes filling with tears. *I didn't even get the chance to say goodbye,* he thought. The book was wrapped with a thin hemp cord, which he untied. Parchment was expensive, and this little book must have cost Carina a small fortune. The inside cover was decorated with runes that Elias did not recognize. There was a folded note

113

tucked into the spine, and Elias pulled it out and recognized Carina's spidery writing.

"My dear Elias, if you are reading this, it means that I am dead, and the time for secrecy is over. Please believe that I only kept things from you for your own safety. I have been working as a spy for King Mitca for nearly forty cycles, well before you were born.

You already know that your mother died during the war, shortly after she gave birth to you. Your mother was Ionela. Your father was Chua, a dragon rider. Some believe that Chua was a traitor—that he betrayed the riders during the war and turned spy for the emperor. I never believed it. You will understand that one day.

I lived among the dwarves for many years. If you ever find yourself with nowhere to go, make your way to Mount Velik. The dwarves will shelter you. They owe me at least that much. This book is my legacy to you. Read it. It holds knowledge of my spells and maps of the land. You have magical abilities—greater than my own. I tried to teach you as best I could without compromising your safety. I wish you would have had a true apprenticeship under an experienced spellcaster, but it was not to be. Study these spells, for the information will likely save your life or the life of someone you love. Be cautious and trust your instincts above all else. I am proud of you, my grandson."

Tears rolled down his cheeks. Elias folded the note and tucked it into his pocket. Then he changed his mind, and opened it, reading it again. *This note is too dangerous for me to keep,* he thought. Although it pained him to do so, he tossed his grandmother's note into the fire, where it burned with blue light. *I'll never be as reckless as I was before. Telling that loudmouth Frogar about the dragon stone cost me everything, but I won't make the same mistake again.*

He flipped through the journal. There were dozens of healing spells, some of which he already knew. There were also a fair number of defensive spells, illusions, and even a few attack spells. *One of these must be the spell that Carina used against the soldiers,* he thought. He vowed to memorize them all, starting with the first. He fell asleep practicing the spells.

Duskeye and Tallin

Back in Parthos, Duskeye and Tallin made the final preparations to leave the Death Sands and fly to the east.

"Are you sure that you want to do this?" asked Sela once again, still surprised that Tallin volunteered for this mission. He was fiercely protective of his dragon and rarely took any risks that put Duskeye in danger.

We are sure, said Duskeye, answering for both of them.

"Please be careful; we can't afford to lose you."

Sela put her hand on Tallin's shoulder briefly. He flinched, unaccustomed to human contact. Sela realized how isolated he must have felt over the years, with only his dragon as his companion. He had forsaken everything—a normal life, friends, children, even a mate, in order to guarantee their survival.

"Don't concern yourself. We're prepared. We'll leave the desert boundary at sunset. We'll be concealed by a cloaking spell for our entire journey. The emperor won't discover us." Tallin tightened the leather saddle and checked his bags. He didn't need much in the way of provisions. Both he and his dragon were accustomed to surviving off the land.

Duskeye nodded, agreeing with his rider, while scratching his pale belly.

Ach! These heavy packs will take some getting used to, said Duskeye. Usually, Tallin rode Duskeye with a simple camel hide. But for this longer journey, they decided to borrow a proper dragon saddle from Sela.

The beautiful saddle was old—and of dwarvish origin. The saddle was made from cowhide and beaten silver. The reins were braided leather and horsehair. There was a protective layer of felted wool between the saddle and the dragon in order to prevent chafing. This saddle was designed for long distances.

Tallin asked the palace servants to bring a few more mealcakes, which he placed into his saddle pack. He stepped into the reins and mounted Duskeye.

"I'll send a message to you when we reach the eastern border. Once we leave the desert, we'll travel only at night. If Chua is alive, we'll find him."

Sela nodded. Tallin was a powerful spellcaster. He could hide in broad daylight and scry at vast distances, something he learned when he lived in the desert. Most of the other dragon riders could scry messages using water, but Tallin was the only one who could scry using smoke, a useful skill when finding a source of water was uncertain.

"Good blessings, Tallin. You, too, Duskeye," she said, patting the dragon's leg.

Thank you, my lady, responded Duskeye. *We shall be careful.*

Duskeye stretched, and then spread his sapphire wings and took flight. Tallin did not look back or wave. He looked straight ahead, staring impassively across the Desert Sands.

They flew in silence for over an hour. Tallin took the time to meditate and rest his mind for the cloaking spell. Tallin was adept at conserving magical energy, and he knew that maintaining the cloaking spell for days would be exhausting.

Are you ready, old friend? asked Duskeye.

"Yes. I'm ready. We're almost at the desert's border. Let's stop at that plateau. I see an overhang that will conceal us. Dusk will fall within the hour, and then we'll cross."

Duskeye landed on the plateau and Tallin dismounted. He drank water and relieved himself. Then dragon and rider sat down in silence and waited for the sun to set. A slight breeze stirred the air, kicking up tiny swirls of red dust.

Dragon and rider watched the magnificent sunset, the sky streaked with purple and yellow light. *I'll miss the beauty of this place,* thought Tallin. This would be their first trip outside the desert in decades.

We'll be back soon, old friend, said Duskeye.

"I know," said Tallin. "Hopefully, we'll return to Parthos with another rider. If Chua is alive, we must find him."

Part Two:
The Escape from Darkmouth Forest

The Gates of Jutland

Elias awoke with a start. He looked around frantically. He had forgotten where he was. The fireplace had puttered out, and there was only ash. He shivered. It was going to be a cold morning.

Thorin was already awake and dressed, crouched by the window.

"Brrr... it's cold in here. Thorin, did it snow again last night?"

"Shhh! Quiet, Elias!" he said, putting a finger to his lips. "I'm listenin' to the conversation outside."

Elias got up and walked to the window. Two food merchants were chattering right outside the door. He could hear bits and pieces of their conversation. Dwarves had exceptional hearing, so Thorin was able to clearly hear everything they said.

"Yup, they came to the gate this morning, asking about a boy," said the first man. "Said the boy was mageborn and Vosper's lookin' for him. The reward's one hundred silver coins to anyone who finds him." The man was short and fat, pulling a cart filled with lemons.

"That's a nice sum. Did they post a notice? What does he look like?"

"That's the problem. Brown hair, brown eyes, but otherwise nobody knows for sure. He looks like half the bloody boys in town! If he's here, they'll find 'im. They brought a necromancer along." The man shivered as he said it.

"Ugh, did you get a good look at 'im? Are their eyes really all black?"

"This one was a female—if you could even call it that. I saw her early this mornin', near Isley's Pub. Her hair was black, her eyes were black, and her teeth were red—and sharpened into points. She laughed at something, and it sounded like a dying buzzard. She near scared me to death!"

"The female necromancers are frightening—more frightening than the males!"

"If you see her, don't look straight at her. She might freeze you to death or lay a curse on you. I tell you, those necromancers make my blood run cold."

The men continued to talk as they made their way to the city square.

Thorin looked up. "This is bad news, Elias. There's no way ye can fight a necromancer and win. She would overpower ye in an instant. We cannot stay in Jutland."

"The emperor sent a necromancer looking for me? But why?" said Elias. "I don't understand this."

"I don't either. But it doesn't matter. We have to leave the city. It's better if we go immediately. Necromancers are more powerful at night. If we try to leave after sunset, she'll find you for sure. We'll leave within the hour. I must tell Floki."

Thorin walked to the bedroom and knocked on the door. Elias heard murmured voices, and then a loud gasp. Halda started weeping again, this time more loudly.

Floki and Thorin walked back out into the living room. "Both of you must go," Floki said grimly. "The best chance you have is to conceal yourselves. They'll be looking for a boy, so you can't leave the city on mounted horseback. We'll load up a cart with hides, and Elias will hide inside the cart. Then you can take the horses and leave the cart outside the city. I'll come back after nightfall and tell the guards that I was robbed by bandits."

"We have to put as much distance as possible between ourselves and the city," said Thorin.

"What can I do to help?" asked Elias.

"Didn't yer grandmother teach ye any concealment spells?" asked Thorin.

"No—no, not really. But I saw one in her journal. I don't know how effective it will be."

"Well, practice it," said Thorin. "Yer simple spell won't stop the necromancer, but it may be enough to fool the guards at the gate."

"I'll start practicing the spell now," said Elias. His grandmother's little book of spells was coming in handy already. Elias walked out to the stable, enjoying the earthy smell of manure and horses. It was welcoming, and it reminded him of home. Thorin had two beautiful stallions and three mares. Elias sat down in a dark corner, opened the precious journal, and started practicing the spell quietly.

***

Thorin and Floki worked fast. Thorin hummed a song quietly under his breath, packing the cart and the horses.

"Thorin, use only the light pack," said Floki. "We want the guards to believe that this is just a daytrip to Gardarsholm."

Halda came outside with some corncakes and dried beef strips. The simple food would sustain them for a few days if they rationed it properly. Her eyes were red from crying.

"Floki, should I start packing our things?" she asked, her voice trembling.

"Yes. We must leave with the children immediately. Don't tell anyone where we're going. You must be ready to leave when I return. Pack rations and our coin purses. It's too dangerous for us to linger in Jutland any longer."

"B-but the baby, Floki..." Halda's lower lip trembled.

"It cannot be helped," he responded, grasping her shoulders. "The emperor hates dwarves almost as much as he hates dragons, and his necromancer won't hesitate to kill all of us. If we stay here, it's only a matter of time before we're questioned and killed. They won't spare our children, Halda. You know this."

Halda nodded, lowering her head. Her eyes streamed with tears. She knew that her husband told the truth. The only safe place for them now was Mount Velik. They had to try and make it there. She didn't blame Thorin and Elias, but it hurt just the same. They had built a life together in Jutland, and now, to be uprooted with so little warning, was painful.

Thorin cleared his throat and coughed politely. "Floki, sorry to interrupt, but the horses are ready to go."

"All right. Parvel!" said Floki, calling again for his young son.

"Yes, Father?" answered Parvel, who came running from inside the house.

"Go find Elias and tell him it's time to get going. He's somewhere in the stables. Don't be too loud, though."

Parvel bolted to the stables, calling Elias' name.

This is my chance to test the spell, Elias thought to himself. He read the runes out loud, carefully, "*Hud-leyna!*" He saw a shimmer in the air, and then it stabilized. He crouched in the corner, in plain sight. The sensation was peculiar—he felt as though he was sitting inside an egg.

Parvel entered the stable and walked back and forth, calling his name. He walked past Elias twice, just inches away from him. He scratched his head quizzically.

"Elias? Are you in here? I can hear you breathing, but I can't see you."

Elias released the spell, frowning. *Blast! Parvel could still sense I was here,* he thought.

"Oh, there you are! Were you spellcasting?" asked Parvel, his eyes as wide as saucers.

"Yes, I was. It didn't work. You could still hear me," Elias said, disappointed.

"No, it worked! I couldn't see you. Remember, I'm part dwarf. My hearing is better than yours. I don't think that a normal human would have heard you."

"That's true, isn't it?" said Elias. "Maybe we'll get lucky at the gate after all."

Parvel and Elias walked out to meet Thorin and Floki.

"Father! Elias cast a hiding spell. I couldn't see him, but he was right in front of me!" said Parvel.

"Aye! That's great news, boy," said Thorin, smiling broadly. "Ye've got the hang of it, then?"

"Yes, but Parvel could still hear me breathing. The spell doesn't mask noise—only my appearance. I can't hold my breath the whole time," said Elias.

"Don't fret. The guards are human. We just have to get past them. How long do you think ye can hold the spell?"

"Thirty minutes, maybe more if I concentrate. It's pretty tiring," said Elias.

"That's plenty of time to get us out of the city and into the forest. Now let's just pray that we don't encounter the necromancer, or our goose is cooked," said Thorin.

Floki nodded grimly. Everyone knew that necromancers could easily detect such a simple spell. If the necromancer appeared at the gate, they would be taken into custody, and Elias would be delivered to the emperor as a prisoner. The necromancer would probably just kill him and Thorin after torturing them for information. Then the soldiers would return to Floki's home and kill his entire family.

Floki sighed. "Thorin, I hate to admit it, but I've gotten comfortable here in Jutland, and I've ignored the warnings for too long. People in Jutland have been skittish and afraid for months. It's been getting worse, and I've just turned a blind eye to the danger. Even if we all made it out of Jutland alive, dark days are ahead."

"Aye. Like it or not, war is comin'," said Thorin.

The Useless Mage

Duskeye and Tallin had been traveling for days. The sun had set many hours ago, and Duskeye was yawning.

Tallin, we should stop and rest, my friend, said Duskeye, communicating silently with his rider. *I see a place where I can land.*

Tallin's face was white with strain. He was exhausted from maintaining his powerful cloaking spell. He had been holding it steady for two days.

"Then we shall stop, my friend. Give me a moment." Tallin closed his eyes and raised his arms. Instantly, mist converged around them and they were shielded by a thick fog. The fog got thicker as they touched down. They were in a heavily forested area with no caves. "We're near the city of Rignus. I recognize the area. There are old growth trees that will conceal us."

Duskeye pointed to a great oak tree with a hollowed trunk. Both of them could just barely squeeze inside.

It's not ideal, but I'll gather some branches to cover the opening. We'll be safe here, said Duskeye.

The dragon collected some downed branches and placed them around the tree and on the opening. Then they both crawled inside, Tallin lying down on top of Duskeye's soft belly.

I'll take the first watch. Sleep, my friend, said Duskeye.

Tallin nodded gratefully; his eyes closed and he was asleep immediately.

***

Tallin, now on watch, could hear men's voices in the distance. "Duskeye! Wake up! Soldiers!" said Tallin, communicating telepathically. The dragon awoke with a snort. It was not yet dawn.

Where are they? asked the dragon.

"I can't see them with my eyes, but I can sense them. They're at the very edge of my cloaking spell. There's a mage with them, but I sense that he's inexperienced. He knows that there's magic here, but he can't identify its origin."

What shall we do? Do you want to attack? I shall make short work of them, snorted Duskeye, licking his lips.

"No, it's too risky," said Tallin. "We could kill them all, but if the emperor is awaiting a message from these fools, then killing them could be dangerous. I'll scale back the cloaking spell and create a circle of protection around us. Hopefully, they'll come our way and we can hear what they say."

Tallin withdrew his spell. As he did so, his dragon stone glowed on his chest with a bluish light.

A few minutes later, about ten soldiers came into view. They were all on horseback, except for a blundering mage who traveled on a black pony. Both the mage and his horse were obese. The mage trailed behind the soldiers, mumbling to himself.

"I told you, I don't feel good about this," said the mage. "We should leave this area. It's not safe here. We're being watched."

"By Golka! What a skillful magician! How did we ever get so lucky? Now someone is spying on us?" snickered one of the soldiers. "You couldn't even lead our horses to water yesterday!"

"I'm serious!" sputtered the mage, who was sweating profusely. He wiped his greasy brow with his sleeve. "There's something here, I'm sure of it."

"You're sure?" asked the captain, but he wasn't laughing. He was angry. "Pangran, tell me honestly—is there a more *useless* mage in the entire kingdom? Can you do anything worthwhile? Anything at all?"

"Hey, Captain—I can think of one thing—he sure knows how to eat! Him and his bloody fat pony!"

All the soldiers laughed and Pangran, the mage, bowed his head with shame. He was obviously a frequent target of the soldiers' mockeries, and he suffered this indignity in silence.

Pangran did not protest any more, but his eyes kept darting back and forth. The mage grew more nervous with each passing moment.

That mage is ridiculous, but he still knows some-thing is wrong, said Duskeye. *He can feel magic here, but he's too embarrassed to say anything else. What a fool.*

"It's nice to know that the emperor's mages have grown fat and lazy," whispered Tallin. "We're lucky that they don't have a necromancer with them." Tallin was grateful that there wasn't a necromancer in the group because they would have been forced to run or fight. They wouldn't have had a choice.

Agreed... although I wouldn't mind testing my skills against one of those filthy deadrats.

Tallin didn't respond. Duskeye was always itching for a fight while Tallin was the cautious one. More than anything, Duskeye enjoyed the hunt. For all their intelligence, dragons were still wild animals. Tallin had kept them safe all these years, and most of their close scrapes had occurred because Duskeye let his guard down.

One of the soldiers kicked his foot against a tree. "Captain, why are we traipsing all over the countryside? To find a teenage boy? The emperor has hundreds of men looking for him, and none of us even knows what he looks like."

"Just do as you're told. We don't get paid to question the emperor's orders. Our job is to find any boy that fits the description and test him for mageborn skills. It's why we're stuck with Pangran," said the captain, jerking his thumb in the direction of the mage. "Although I don't know if he can even do that."

The mage found this particular comment offensive, and he raised his chin and sniffed loudly. "Captain, I resent that statement. I am perfectly capable of testing a mage-born child!"

Some of the men laughed, but Pangran wasn't letting the subject go. "I've had enough of your harassment! You would do well to show me some respect!" the mage yelled, and his hands started to glow.

"Aye, look at 'im! What are you going to do, 'eh? Throw a firecracker at us? Shut up, you slobbering fool, before I punch your face in!" said one of the men, and now all the other soldiers joined in, laughing and snickering.

"Do you think that you could cast a spell and make yourself disappear? That would make everyone happy," said another. This caused an eruption of laughter that lasted several minutes.

Pangran's face turned red. His anxiety and the soldiers' constant ribbing had finally taken its toll. His right hand glowed, and a small ball of flame formed in his palm. "This is the last time you will disrespect me! *Hringr-Incêndio!*" he yelled.

The captain's eyes widened, and he jumped up to stop the mage, but it was too late. Pangran's flabby arm reached back, and he threw the fireball at the men. His aim was poor, and the men scattered. The fireball flew towards the oak tree where Tallin and Duskeye were hiding. Rather than striking the tree, the fireball dissipated in a shimmer. Tallin's heart skipped a beat.

"What the—look out! It's a protection spell!" the captain barked.

Tallin's spell stopped the fireball easily, but now they were exposed.

"Here we go," he said.

Good! I was itching for a fight! Duskeye smiled widely, his forked tongue moving under his teeth. There was going to be a fight after all!

The fat mage turned white, raising his hands to create a bubble around them, but it was too late. Duskeye and Tallin tore aside the branches, and Duskeye roared. It was so loud that the ground shook. Tallin drew his sword—a short falchion with a leather-wrapped hilt.

"It's a dragon rider! Run—run for your lives!" screamed the panicked mage as he jumped on his pony and turned tail into the forest.

The horses scattered, and the men shouted in alarm. Most of them were young, and they had never seen a dragon. Duskeye's massive jaw opened and white fire came out, burning two of the men where they stood.

"Feel our wrath, dragonkillers!" yelled Tallin.

Tallin struck one man with a paralyzing spell, and he collapsed onto the ground in convulsions. Another soldier surprised him from behind, swinging a broadsword. Tallin didn't have time to deflect, and the sword grazed his right shoulder. Tallin winced, grabbing his injured arm. Duskeye felt Tallin's pain through the dragon stone and swung his tail, striking the soldier's torso. The man flew high into the air and struck a tree. He crumpled to the ground, unconscious.

Two more soldiers attacked Tallin from the front, driving him back into the tree. Both soldiers aimed for his injured arm. Tallin blocked the blows with his sword, ducked his head, and swung to the left, while grabbing a dagger from his wristband. Tallin spun on the ball of his foot, throwing the dagger deep into the eye of the first soldier. The man fell backwards, screaming.

"Duskeye! Your right side!" said Tallin. Duskeye's right eye was blind, and the soldiers struck his leg. Duskeye breathed fire again, but the soldiers stepped back. None of them were hit by the flames the second time.

Tallin jumped high into the air and swung downward with his blade, hitting another soldier in the neck. A fountain of blood erupted from the wound, and the man fell. Another soldier engaged him from the right, and Tallin deflected the blow, but lost his balance. He fell and rolled back, jumping up to defend himself against more assailants. Tallin held his own, but these men were well-trained. Eventually, he would be overpowered. Tallin reached out and communicated with his dragon. "Duskeye—there are too many of them, and these are experienced fighters. I can't concentrate well enough to overpower them all! I need you to fly us out of here!"

Duskeye swung his tail furiously, but he had already sustained several cuts. He couldn't see well enough to safeguard his right side. Duskeye nodded, and Tallin scrambled up on his dragon's back. The soldiers continued to attack, and they hit Duskeye's injured leg again and again. Even though the dragon's scales offered some protection, blood flowed from the wounds. Duskeye kicked off and flew up into the air about twenty feet. "Stop," ordered Tallin. "That's far enough."

"*Nagl-meizi!*" cried Tallin. At first nothing happened. Then tiny pebbles swirled up from the ground, glowing white. The soldiers looked on, bewildered. Tallin began to rotate his wrists furiously, and the pebbles also began to spin. They looked like miniature hurricanes, glowing and spinning up with dust.

"Ow!" cried one of the soldiers as a pebble hit him. Then he screamed, "The rocks are burning hot! They're burrowing into my skin!"

Tallin kept spinning his wrists, faster and faster, and the little hurricanes spun hotter and faster as well. The men didn't even have a chance to run. The heated rocks shredded their armor and clothing—and sizzled through their skin. "Augggh! Augggh! They're burning my chest!" The screams of the soldiers echoed through the forest. The men jerked and scratched at their clothing, but it was no use. Within seconds, they had collapsed.

"Is that all of them?" asked Tallin, breathing heavily.

I believe so. The only one missing is that fat mage.

Duskeye settled back down onto the ground, and Tallin exhaled deeply. The spell had drained him, and he still had to heal Duskeye's wounds. Tallin paused for a moment to gather his strength, and he touched Duskeye's wounded leg, healing the cuts.

Thank you, my friend. Now... let's go find that mage, said Duskeye.

"Yes," Tallin replied. He mounted Duskeye and they took flight, flying low, just above the trees. All dragons can perceive magical energy, and Duskeye concentrated, using his senses to find the escaped mage.

"I bet he's trying to generate a cloaking spell right now," said Tallin.

A lot of good that will do him! I could find this human just based on his awful smell. He's a sweaty, pungent one.

Tallin chuckled. They kept searching, and eventually they found the mage and his pony cowering underneath some thick brambles. Tallin dismounted and pulled Pangran out of the brambles by his collar. Duskeye grabbed the pony in his jaws and cracked its neck with a loud snap. Then he tore it apart and ate it in a few gulps.

The mage screamed while Duskeye devoured the pony.

Delicious! Horses aren't usually my preference, but this one was fantastic, marbled with fat. The dragon burped, satisfied. Then he sat back on his haunches to watch his rider interrogate the terrified mage.

Tallin hated the emperor's mages. To him, they were all traitors. He shook the fat mage violently by the neck. "You! Tell me what you're doing here, and I might let you live."

"I can't! I-I can't! The emperor will kill me!" he whimpered.

"The emperor isn't here, and all your men are dead. You should be more worried about what I'm going to do to you. Talk now, or my dragon will roast you alive... slowly."

The mage gulped. "I—I don't know much. The emperor is sending men all over the countryside, trying to find some mageborn boy. His name is Ellis, or Elias— something like that."

Tallin shook him again. "What else?"

"V-Vosper is using his own necromancers to find the boy. He rarely lets any of them leave Morholt, so that means that this mission is very important to the emperor."

"I see," said Tallin. "Anything else?"

"I don't know anything more than that. I don't even know why Vosper is looking for him—our orders are just to bring him back alive. Any mageborn that fits the description must be delivered to the capital. That's all I know, I swear! By Golka, please let me go!" pleaded the mage, clasping his hands. Tallin released his collar and the mage fell to his knees, coughing.

"Get up, you fool. Die like a man," said Tallin gravely.

"What? B-but you promised! You said you would let me live!"

"I never promised you anything. You deserve to die. You're a coward and a traitor. Those soldiers never had a chance, but you didn't even try to protect them. I know that you'll betray us to the emperor the first chance you get. Be thankful that I'm giving you a painless death. It's more than you deserve."

"No—no—please, don't! I won't say anything, I swear!" he pleaded, but it was already too late. Duskeye's clawed hand shot out and severed the man's spine. His back arched, and he made a gurgling noise. The mage was dead before his face hit the ground. Tallin resisted the urge to kick him.

"This mage was a weak-minded fool. Is this the type of spellcaster that the empire is producing?"

Perhaps. The emperor can't really afford to have powerful spellcasters in Morholt. What if they rose against him? Just having necromancers is risky enough.

"True. Who knows what Vosper intends to do? It's impossible to know his motivations. Duskeye, we have to cover the evidence. Burn this part of the forest," said Tallin. "I'll call a messenger and send word to Mitca. He must be warned. Things are accelerating faster than I expected."

Tallin whistled for a messenger. He thought about sending a message back to Sela, but decided against it. He needed to conserve his strength and attempting a telepathic message at such a long distance would drain his already depleted reserves.

A few minutes later, a huge black crow landed on Tallin's shoulder. Tallin reached up and gently touched its head with his thumb.

"How are you this evening, old friend?"

The bird cawed loudly in reply. Tallin smiled. He loved these intelligent scavengers. When he first became a dragon rider, bird-language was one of the things that fascinated him the most. He spent hours listening to their intricate songs and playful chatter.

Tallin pulled out a snippet of parchment from his pocket and scorched a magical message into the paper.

"Warning: the emperor knows about the boy. He is sending out necromancers. We are crossing into Darkmouth Forest in three days. We go to the Elder Willow."

The parchment smoked as the runes appeared and then immediately vanished. He rolled the parchment into a little scroll and attached it to the crow's foot. He whispered his instructions to the crow, who squawked a response in primitive bird language.

As an afterthought, Tallin reached down and plucked out the dead mage's eyes, offering them to the crow. The bird swallowed the eyes greedily and took flight. The crow would reach the Death Sands in three days, maybe four.

Tallin looked over his shoulder, feeling the heat from the spreading flames. Duskeye was magnificent. A river of white flame poured from his mouth, burning everything in its path. The fire spread, and soon the entire forest was burning, destroying evidence of the dead soldiers and their cowardly mage with it.

The Necromancer

Thorin and Floki covered Elias with hides and attached the cart to one of the mares. They were ready to leave the city.

"Elias, stay alert," said Floki. "Save your strength, and use the concealment spell only if we're stopped along the way. I'll tap the side of the cart twice once we get to the guardpost. We'll be searched at the gate, so make sure you hide yourself once we get there."

"I'll ride ahead and make sure that the necromancer isn't at the gate," Thorin said. "I suspect that it's resting now. Necromancers tire easily during the day. Their vision and strength is much better at night."

Elias memorized the concealment spell, but he was still nervous. He could not afford to make a mistake. He heard the stable gate click, and they started to travel towards the city exit. His stomach felt unsettled. He regretted not eating breakfast.

As they rode through the city, Thorin took stock of all the activity. There were fewer merchants on the streets today, and many of the shops were closed. Word traveled fast—people were staying inside because of the necromancer. As they reached the city gate, Thorin and Floki both breathed a sigh of relief. The necromancer was nowhere in sight.

The line to leave the city was long because all the carts and carriages were being searched. The regular city guards were there, but there were also two empire soldiers. They sat on horseback in leather armor, yellow plumes from their silver helmets glinting in the sunlight.

People chattered in line, although more quietly than usual. The two soldiers watched the activity silently from either side of the gate.

One of the merchants at the front of the line started arguing with one of the guards. "Hurry up, ye daft fools! I'll never make it to Faerroe by tomorrow if ye keep harrassin' me horses and me goods!"

"Be patient. We'll be done soon enough, old man," said the guard, who continued to look through all the merchant's bags.

The merchant complained louder. "This is outrageous! What in blazes are ye lookin' fer? I don't have nothin' ye need!" he shouted again.

One of the soldiers frowned. He'd heard enough. The old man was turned away from the soldier, who drew his sword. The crowd gasped. The soldier smacked the merchant in the back of the head with the flat of his sword, and the man went down, face first into the mud.

"Confiscate his goods and take him away. We do not have the patience for this," said the soldier. Then he addressed the line. "Does anyone else have any… grievances? Anyone?"

The people fell silent and looked away.

"Good," said the soldier, sheathing his sword. "We can move a lot faster if everyone cooperates. If not, then you'll get the same treatment as our ill-tempered old friend."

A city guardsman dragged the unconscious merchant out of the way, and his donkey cart was moved off to the side.

Thorin looked at Floki, but said nothing. It took another miserable hour, standing in drizzle, to get up to the gate. One of the regular guards recognized Floki. "Aye, Floki, where are you goin'?"

"I'm going to Gardarsholm to meet another merchant. He wants to purchase some of my premium leathers. That's what I have in the cart." Floki tapped the cart twice, and Elias said the cloaking spell quietly.

"All right then. I need to search the cart before you leave."

Floki lifted the tarp covering the hides, and the soldiers nodded in silent approval. They saw nothing but hides. Floki smiled, replaced the tarp, and dug his heels into his horse. The horse started trotting towards the gate. They were almost through when he heard a shriek, like the sound of breaking glass.

"Sssstop!" screeched a cloaked figure, as it glided down from the watchtower. The necromancer! She had been watching from above all along.

Long black hair spilled out from underneath her hood. Her skin was alabaster white, but her lips were very red. She reached out and grabbed Floki's chin. "Sssssssso… what do we have here? A dwarf half-ling, eh?" her voice rasped.

Floki stiffened, but he stood his ground. "Yes. I am." He jerked his chin out of her grip and touched the dagger strapped to his belt. The necromancer laughed, revealing two rows of red, sharpened teeth.

"Sssssss… What are you planning to do with that little knife of yours, hmmmm? Do you plan to fight me, half-brrrreed?" Then she turned to Thorin, who was a few people behind in line. "And how about you, old dwarf? Did you think that I didn't see you, ssssticking out like a sssssore thumb?"

Thorin just stared calmly. His face betrayed no emotion. "A good day to you, dark one."

The necromancer snorted in reply, turning her attention back to Floki. She lifted the tarp up again and sniffed inside. Nothing was visible except the hides. The necromancer paused and sniffed again. Floki held his breath. His hand tightened around the dagger.

She closed her black eyes and backed away. "You may leave, half-ling. Take your cart of leathers." Then she looked squarely at Thorin. "You! Old dwarf… get out. Don't let me catch you back insssside this city… or I'll gut you… from nose to navel."

Thorin bowed slightly and trotted away on Duster, humming quietly as usual. He joined Floki on the road, but they did not speak until they were a league from the city.

"Floki, take a breath. Have ye been holdin' it in the whole time?" Thorin chuckled.

Floki exhaled deeply and said, "By Baghra! That necromancer scared me nearly to death! I felt its breath on me and it was freezing cold. That thing isn't even human!"

"You're right. It isn't. Floki, there's no reason to be afraid of something that you can't control. She was either going to kill us, or she was going to let us go. Lucky for us, she decided to let us go."

"Is it okay for me to come out yet?" said Elias, muffled underneath the tarp. "It's hot under here!"

Thorin replied without turning around. "Not yet, boy. It's too dangerous. I can still see the city behind us. Just be patient. We'll be in Darkmouth Forest soon enough, and then ye can come out. Keep up the spell as long as ye can, just in case."

"Okay," Elias said.

They traveled another hour before stopping by a small creek. The horses were allowed to drink, and Thorin dismounted.

"Come on out, boy," said Thorin, pulling back the tarp. "We're going to pause here for a moment, and then we'll continue on our way."

The air shimmered, and Elias appeared, exhaling loudly. "Finally! I didn't know how much longer I could hold that spell. I felt fine this morning, but holding it steady for so long drained my energy."

"Cloakin' spells are difficult to maintain, even simple ones like yers," said Thorin. "The more ye practice, the easier it will become. Keep trainin', because it's likely that ye will have to use it again."

"How do you know so much about magic, Thorin?" asked Elias.

"Boy, I'm much older than I look. I've seen plenty of wars in me day, and there's another one comin', ye can be sure of that. Best be prepared, I say." Thorin smiled and started humming again. Elias was speechless. Nothing seemed to faze him.

"Floki, are you going to travel with us any farther?" asked Elias.

"No. I'm going to wait here and see if there's anyone I know returning to the city. I might get lucky and get a message to my family without having to return. If that deadrat is still at the gate, I'll probably be arrested if I try to reenter. But either way, I must fetch my family. It's not safe for any of us to remain here," said Floki. "Thorin, I've decided to go back to Mount Velik. It's best for all of us."

"I'm sorry, old friend," said Thorin, placing his hand on Floki's shoulder. "I know it was a hard decision for ye. I'll be expectin' ye soon at Mount Velik, cousin. When ye arrive, we'll have a feast waitin' for ye. May the gods protect ye and yer family on the journey."

Floki clasped Thorin's hand. They were silent for a moment. Elias turned away; he felt partly responsible for the predicament that Floki was in.

Floki walked over to his horse, a pretty chestnut mare. "Take care of Buttercup, boy. She's yours now. She's a fine horse and as good natured as any I've ever owned."

"I will... I promise," said Elias quietly.

"And listen to Thorin. If anyone can get you out of the trouble you're in, it's him. Take a few hides from the cart; they'll come in handy while you're traveling. Good luck to you both. Now go, before it's too late. You should try to be as far away from Jutland as possible by nightfall."

Thorin unhooked the cart from Buttercup's saddle, and Elias mounted the mare. Together, Thorin and Elias left the clearing. Elias turned back around. He saw Floki sitting on the cart, shoulders hunched, with his head in his hands. What if Floki's family was killed because of him? Elias turned back around, sighing heavily.

"Don't be blamin' yerself, lad. Everything will be all right in time. Just have a wee bit of faith," Thorin said, staring straight ahead. "Why don't ye pull out that spell book of yers? Practicin' those spells is going be more helpful than cryin'."

Elias wiped his nose with his tunic sleeve. Thorin was right. There was no point in getting upset now. He had to be strong. He owed it to his grandmother, and he owed it to Thorin. He pulled the little journal out of his pack and started reading.

"That's a clever lad," said Thorin, smiling. "We've got a few days of travel before we're out of this forest, so ye may as well learn somethin' useful along the way."

A few minutes later, Thorin started to hum quietly. Elias smiled. Thorin's positive attitude was infectious. They rode on at a steady pace, keeping off the main path.

Elias flipped to the map in his grandmother's journal. They were traveling east. If they traveled fast, they might make it to Faerroe by tomorrow evening. From there, it was at least five days by horseback to reach the Orvasse River.

That's if they made it out of Faerroe alive.

Mitca's Bad News

Back in Parthos, Sela paced nervously in the corridor, waiting for King Mitca to arrive. A few moments later, one of the king's guards popped his head through the thick curtains outside the chamber.

"Mistress Sela, you may enter."

"Thank you," she replied. She handed the guard her dagger and short sword. Even the dragon riders were prohibited from wearing their weapons in the king's throne room.

"Sela, thank you for coming to speak with me in private," said the king. "Please sit."

Sela took a seat at the table, and the king stepped down to join her. There was a bowl of fruit on the table, and she picked absently at some grapes. Her heart pounded with emotion. Even though years had passed since they were lovers, it still made her uncomfortable to be alone with the king.

The other dragon riders did not know that Sela and Mitca were past lovers, although Tallin suspected something and told her as much. Sela denied the relationship, but her face betrayed her true emotions. It was impossible to keep anything secret from Tallin. He seemed to know everything about everyone.

"Sela, this is not a social call," said Mitca.

"I know," Sela replied. "I've been reading the reports from all over Durn. The news is discouraging. Even the dwarves are preparing for battle."

"How goes the training?" asked Mitca.

"Not very well. Riona and Stormshard are too headstrong. Hanko and Charlight are skittish, and Tallin and Duskeye are uncontrollable. Karela and Orshek may never be ready to take a rider. Their training goes slowly. It's... disheartening."

"Then you must work harder. Accelerate their training. All of the riders have to be ready for war, and time is a luxury we can no longer afford. The emperor's armies are gathering in the east. Parthos is no longer safe. I lost six of my best soldiers last week to a Balborite assassin."

"Another one? That's the second one this year," said Sela.

"Actually, it was the third. You and Brinsop killed one, and Tallin and Duskeye found another traveling alone in the desert. This most recent attack actually reached the city gates. Three of my guards fell instantly, and two others were stabbed with daggers laced with kudu oil. One of my captains managed to remove the dagger in his arm and stab the assassin. Only minutes later, they both died in convulsions from the poison. Neither wound would have been fatal otherwise."

"Why didn't I hear of these other attacks?" Sela pounded her fist on the table. "It's my job to keep the city safe!"

King Mitca stared coldly at Sela. "A king must keep his own counsel. I did not want anyone to panic. I do not presume to be told how to do my job, even by a dragon rider."

Sela hung her head, chastised. "My lord—how can I prepare for future attacks if I'm not allowed to study the enemy?"

"All of the assassins were killed. You know that a Balborite can never be taken alive. Tallin and Duskeye captured the one they found, but he was dead before they returned to the city. The assassin committed suicide along the way, without using any weapons."

"Did the assassin poison himself?"

"Duskeye carried the body back to the palace so we could examine it. My surgeon performed an autopsy."

"What did he discover?"

"The assassin's flesh was marked everywhere with magical tattoos. Wherever there was a tattoo on the skin, the surgeon's knife could not enter the flesh. Tallin had to intervene. He cast a spell to pierce it. When the doctor opened the assassin's chest, we saw that the heart had burst. It was shattered within his chest. And directly above it was a black stone, implanted near the sternum."

"A runestone!"

"Yes, it was a runestone, enchanted with black magic. I had never seen one up close. Tallin told me not to touch it because the enchantment could still be active. We were able to make the runes visible, but neither Duskeye nor Tallin could decipher the spell. The stone bore an inscription in the Balborite language. That is all that we know. It is unlikely we will ever take any of the Balborite mercenaries alive—they cannot risk anyone deciphering their secrets."

"The runestone blew a hole in the assassin's chest?"

"Yes. As long as the assassins are conscious and able to speak, they will be able to kill themselves to evade capture. I had the ashes of the other assassin examined, and we found an identical runestone in the remains."

"How about if we use a sleeping spell or a para-lyzing agent? If the assassin can't talk, then he can't voice the enchantment. We could capture him alive."

"Yes, it is possible that would work—but to what end? How are we going to question him? As soon as we grant him the ability to speak, he will use the spell to activate the runestone."

Sela sighed. "You have a point. Do you feel the danger has escalated?"

"Yes, definitely. My scouts have returned with grim news from all across Durn. The emperor has started conscripting youths for his army, and he is using outside mercenaries."

"This is old news. The emperor has been assembling troops for over a year. What has changed?"

"It is not what you think. The mercenaries are orcs."

Sela gasped. "Orcs? The emperor is using orcs? That's absurd! Orcs eat humans!"

"Yes, I know. Presumably, the emperor signed a treaty with the orc leader, King Nar, last winter. The orcs have been growing their number for years. Their main outpost is in the northwestern part of Durn in the caves of Mount Heldeofol. King Nar has been waiting for years to get his revenge against the dwarves. Presumably, the emperor has offered Mount Velik as spoils of war if the orcs help him."

"Even the emperor's army will refuse to fight alongside those monsters."

"They won't have to. Look at their positions." Mitca pointed to a large map on the wall. "The emperor plans to flank our city and attack us from the north and the east. It is also likely that he will hire mercenaries from Balbor to attack us from the west. The emperor wants Parthos destroyed at all costs."

"But why now?"

"The prophesy. Once I received the note about the dragon stone, I knew that things had gotten serious. The emperor knows that we are harboring dragon riders. He wants to make sure all of them are killed, even if it means he has to work with orcs in order to do it. He has entered into this unholy alliance as a last resort."

Sela sighed. This was truly alarming news. "Mitca, if orcs capture this city, everyone will die. The greenskins will slaughter every man, woman, and child."

"I know. That is why we have to make sure it does not happen. I have already sent a messenger to the dwarf king, Hergung. We have had a strained relationship until now, but we have little choice but to work together. He has already responded in the affirmative."

"What are your orders?"

"Brief the other dragon riders, but do not tell anyone else. You have one month to finish their training. After that, I will be sending each of you out to collect information and perform certain tasks. Orshek and Karela will stay behind to guard the city."

"Orshek and Karela? But they're too young—and who will communicate with them?" asked Sela.

"One of the palace mages, Alboline, can speak some dragon tongue. She will train alongside them so she can practice. The dragon riders are my best defense inside the Death Sands, but I cannot afford to keep you here any longer. You have to go out and collect information. No one else can travel as fast or as far."

"How about the elves?"

"The elves care little about human suffering. They live out their immortal lives in enchanted cities, and that is where they shall remain. They did not come to our aid during the Orc Wars. Why would they intervene now?"

Sela hung her head. Mitca was right. An alliance with the dwarves was their only hope. If Emperor Vosper had already formed an alliance with the orcs, then they had to move as quickly as possible. Parthos and all of its citizens were in grave danger.

Sela rubbed her temples. She had a pounding headache. She could feel the tendrils of Brinsop's consciousness. Her dragon knew that something was wrong, and he was already waiting on the fortress ramparts for her.

"I hear and obey, my king." Sela ended their conversation formally, and walked out of the throne room.

Mitca heard Sela's soft footfalls as she left the chamber. This was the greatest threat that his city had ever faced. How was he going to tell his people?

Faerroe, City of Thieves

horin and Elias had been riding for two days when they finally reached the city of Faerroe. The city itself was about half the size of Jutland. From the outside, the cities looked similar, but that is where the similarities ended. Disfigured beggars lined the road up to the city gates, crying out with their hands extended.

"Thorin, what has happened to all of these poor people?" Elias whispered in shock. He had never seen anything like it.

"They're vagrants. Faerroe is burstin' with them. Thieves, too. This city isn't safe, even during the day. So watch yerself. Most of the city's inhabitants are involved in black market smugglin'."

Thorin and Elias walked into Faerroe unchallenged. There was one fat guard at the gate, drinking steaming liquid from a grimy cup. The guard nodded at them as they entered, but otherwise said nothing. Greasy black smoke belched from stovepipes, and raw sewage filled the polluted stream running through the city.

At one point, a beggar grabbed Elias' saddle bag and tried to empty its contents. Thorin leaned over and rapped the beggar's knuckles with his knife handle.

"Shoo! Go away!" he scolded.

The beggar glared, rubbing his sore fingers. He made an obscene gesture, and then skulked away.

"Thorin, why are we coming here? Can't we just go around this city?"

"I need information, and I have an important contact here. We need to find out if it's safe to take the Orvasse River up to Mount Velik. If not, we'll have to go by the coastline, which will add weeks to our journey. My friend will know if it's safe to travel the river. He's a smuggler, but an honest smuggler."

"How could someone possibly be an 'honest' smuggler?"

"You'll see what I mean when you meet him," said Thorin, smiling. He seemed unperturbed by all of the filth and beggars.

As they made their way into the city, Elias noticed some merchants on the streets; most were selling prepared food. Some of it was highly questionable. One man offered fresh rabbit, but Elias thought that the skinned carcasses looked suspiciously like cats.

Another sold fried dough, cooked in hot grease. The man kept chasing away children, all of whom looked like they were starving. At one point, a child kicked the man in the shins, and he gave chase down the block, which was just enough time for a tiny accomplice to steal a few pieces of cooked dough.

Elias smiled. He was glad these boys were able to get some food. He could see these people were desperate. Poverty and squalor were everywhere. He and Thorin rode deeper into the city, which didn't seem to improve. After a while, they stopped in front of a plain house with an iron gate out front. It was two stories with peeling blue paint. Thorin banged on the gate and called out, "Aye! Aye! Falenrith!"

A moment later, a thin man poked his head out of the curtains upstairs. "Who is making all that racket?" Then he paused. "Thorin? Thorin Ulfarsson? Is that you?"

"Aye, it is," he replied.

"I'll be right down," the thin man replied. They heard a series of latches being opened, and Falenrith swung open the gate. He was tall, with dark hair and a sparse goatee.

"How are you, old stonebreaker? It's good to see you again." Falenrith bent down and grabbed Thorin in a rough embrace. "Come in, come in. My daughter has just finished making some flatcakes. We can talk over dinner."

"That would be fine, old friend. That would be just fine," said Thorin.

They walked up the stairs and into a small kitchen. Thorin sat down on a stool. Then he pulled his pipe out of his pocket and started to smoke.

A young girl kneeled by the hearth, cooking some flattened bread on a heated stone. A boy, about the same age, was carving a block of wood in the corner. The children both looked to be about twelve years old. They were all very thin, just like their father.

"This is Abby and Braden, my twins." The children waved, but did not say anything. "Abby, please cook a few extra flatcakes for our guests, and get us all a cup of tea."

Abby poured Thorin and Elias each a mug of hot tea. "Thank ye, lass," said Thorin, accepting the cup. A few minutes later, she gave them both two flatcakes, and they settled down on woven mats in the kitchen to eat.

"So, Thorin, I haven't seen you in years. What are you doing in a place like Faerroe?"

"I came to see ye, old friend. Do ye still manage the Shadow Grid?"

Falenrith grimaced. "Abby and Braden, please go to your rooms. We must speak in private." Then his voice dropped to a whisper. "Thorin, how can you come out and just ask me about this? Who is this boy? I don't know him, and I'm not even sure if I trust you!"

"I'm sorry to be so frank with ye. But we've got a necromancer chasin' us, and we really don't have time to be delicate."

"A necromancer?" Falenrith sucked in a quick breath. "Are you sure?"

"I peered into its black eyes myself. It was in Jutland, searching for Elias. This boy is Carina's grandson."

"Carina's grandson?" Falenrith groaned. "Then it's begun. I knew that it would happen sometime, but I just didn't know when."

"What are you both talking about?" asked Elias. He was getting tired of everyone talking about him like he wasn't present.

"Elias, Falenrith used to be a leader in the Shadow Grid. The Shadow Grid was a network of thieves and spies that worked for the resistance," explained Thorin. "The thieves in the Grid are unique because they're all mage-born, and none of them work for the empire."

Elias' eyes widened. "A whole network of free mages? Why, that's great!"

"Sorry to be the bearer of bad news, son, but the Grid is not a network of free mages… as much as a network of starving ones." Falenrith turned to Thorin. "Things have changed since we spoke last. The Grid has disbanded. The emperor captured or killed most of us. I estimate that less than a dozen remain. I don't really know for sure. I've been in hiding in Faerroe for over five years, and I haven't cast a single spell in that time. I still do some smuggling. Textiles, mostly. I try to avoid calling any attention to my family. After Muriel was killed…" Falenrith's voice broke "I lost the will to fight. I've been raising Abby and Braden on my own here. It's been difficult, but at least I feel safe."

"You feel safe in Faerroe?" asked Elias incredulously.

"Yes. The city itself is awful, but I've never seen an empire soldier in all the years I've lived here. The management of the city is such a catastrophe that we hide in plain sight."

"Oh, that makes sense," Elias responded.

Thorin leaned forward, patting Falenrith's knee. "I'm sorry for your loss, old friend. Muriel was a good mage and a fine woman. But ye can't stay here. Ye can't. The empire is coming. Soldiers will come here, probably within the next few days. Ye'll do best to leave the city by tomorrow."

"I don't need your advice, old man," Falenrith snapped. "In fact, I'm tired of bad news. That's all I hear."

"My advice was well-meant, old friend. You would do well to listen," said Thorin.

"Is that why you came here? To give me a warning?" asked Falenrith.

"No. I came because we need information. We need to know if travel on the river is safe."

"How would I know that?"

"Well, I knew that ye handled the smuggling routes. At least ye did years ago. But if ye know nothin', then we'd best be on our way," said Thorin, rising from his chair. This conversation was going nowhere.

"Okay, okay... Wait. Just wait." Falenrith raised his hand and sighed. "I'm sorry. It's just been so hard these last few years. I shouldn't have snapped at you. As for the river—you can still travel down the Orvasse River. I also know something else. At the time, the information... it seemed impossible. I thought it was a mistake."

"What is it?" asked Thorin.

"A few weeks ago, I got a cryptic message from Norgul. He's living up north, studying with the free mages in Miklagard. They use bird messengers to monitor the travel routes up there. He said that there has been a lot of military activity near Mount Heldeofol."

"Isn't that the orc kingdom?" Elias asked.

Thorin's expression remained calm as always, but Elias saw Thorin's lips twitch.

"Yes, it is," replied Falenrith. "Norgul intercepted a message from one of Vosper's couriers, but they couldn't decipher it. The only thing they knew for certain was that the message was from the emperor. It couldn't have been a forgery. The emperor's seal was unbroken."

"The dwarves also heard rumors, but didn't believe it either," said Thorin. "Then there's no doubt. The emperor is communicating with King Nar."

"Who is King Nar?" asked Elias.

"The orc king. He's been wantin' to get his revenge on the dwarf clans for a long time," said Thorin. "If Vosper forms an alliance with the greenskins, then the entire continent is at risk. Orcs have no sense of morality or decency. They'll kill everythin' in their path. I would not have imagined it, but if this is true, then the emperor has truly gone mad."

Thorin turned to Elias and leaned over to whisper in his ear. "Elias, we must return to Mount Velik at once. Our lives are in more danger than I originally predicted. I'm sorry, but we won't be going to the Elder Willow."

"Is it safe for us to travel?" asked Elias.

"Take the Orvasse River. It's safe," said Falenrith. "I have a friend who charters boats at Hwīt Rock. If you make it to the outpost, then he'll transport you to Mount Velik. The captain's name is Gremley and his boat is the Chipperwick. He's smart and fair, and he doesn't ask too many questions. He'll even smuggle goods, as long as you pay him and keep quiet. He knows the Orvasse River better than anyone else at the outpost."

"I believe I've met Gremley," said Thorin, scratching his chin. "I purchased a passage from him over a dozen years ago—he might remember me still."

"Just tell him that I sent you and that you wish to go to Ironport. That's only a few leagues from Mount Velik, and it won't arouse any suspicion."

"It's settled then. We'll head towards the Orvasse River tonight. Once we get to Hwīt Rock, we'll charter a boat and travel to Mount Velik," said Thorin. "It's the fastest way."

Falenrith stood up and shook their hands. "Good luck to you both. I'm sorry I couldn't be of more help."

"What will you do?" Elias asked Falenrith.

He shrugged. "I'm not sure. We've moved before, and under greater duress than this. We can't go east—the emperor will kill us. If we're lucky, we might make it to Miklagard alive. We'll have to travel over the mountains and through Lockdell Barrens, so we'll have to wait until the weather improves. If we leave Faerroe, we might be able to stay farther south.

"I have an aunt in Starryford." Falenrith paused and ran his hand through his hair. "I must go tell my children. You can let yourselves out." He turned and walked out of the room.

"He's upset, Thorin," said Elias.

"I know it. I expected him to be. No one likes to hear bad news. It's better that he finds out now. At least he can make an educated decision. The emperor has been searchin' for him for years, and there's still an active bounty for his head."

Elias peeked around the corner and saw Falenrith talking quietly to his children. They looked so thin and fragile.

"Let's go, boy. We've worn out our welcome here," said Thorin quietly. "We've got to get out of Faerroe. There's some hard day's ridin' ahead for us."

It seems like hard days are ahead for all of us, thought Elias.

The Night Visitor

Elias and Thorin rode hard for the next three days. They ate in their saddles and only paused to relieve themselves and to allow the horses to drink. They kept off the regular road, and Elias used a concealment spell whenever they saw other travelers. They slept very little, stopping only a few hours. They rose before the sunrise to continue on again.

On the third day, Thorin paused and pointed into the distance. "See that outcropping of rock? That's Hwīt Rock. There's a trading post there, and boats for hire. We've got at least another full day of hard ridin' before we reach it. We'll keep goin' until the light fades, and then we'll make camp. The horses must rest."

Elias nodded. His mare had flecks of white spittle around her mouth. He patted her neck soothingly and whispered in her ear, "I know you're tired, old girl, but we're almost there." They were all exhausted.

They rode on until nightfall and then Thorin stopped and dismounted. There was a spring nearby and the horses drank water and started to graze. "Here's a good a place as any. We can't risk lightin' a fire, so why don't you just lie down and rest? I'll take the first watch."

Elias nodded and pulled out one of the hides. It was stiff, but he was grateful for it because the ground was still pretty wet and cold. He propped himself up against a tree and started eating a piece of flatbread. This was the last of their rations, but both of them were too tired to hunt.

"Thorin, how long will it take for us to get to Mount Velik once we reach the river?"

"About three days if we get a speedy vessel. Perhaps four. We don't want to be sailin' past the capital city during the day. The emperor has defensive posts on both sides of the river. We shouldn't compromise safety for speed, but I won't know for sure until we reach the river."

As the last of the light faded, Elias pulled out a white crystal from his pocket. "*Liuhath!*" he whispered, and the crystal glowed with warm blue light.

Thorin smiled. "That's a neat little trick, boy."

"It will stay lit all night. It's one of the first spells I learned. The crystal holds the energy of the spell, so it lasts a long time without draining my energy. My grandmother used crystals to store magical energy, but I never really learned how to do it. This is the only crystal spell I know."

"Crystal magic is a disappearing art, boy. There aren't many proficient at it anymore because it takes so long to learn."

"Do any of the dwarf mages practice crystal magic?"

"Only a few in our history, and only one that I know of who is still alive. He is old, much older than I. There are only a half dozen dwarf mages at Mount Velik. It's not a common gift for our people. Usually, the mageborn trait is passed down from a human ancestor, or, more rarely, from one who has elven blood."

"There are dwarves with elven blood?" asked Elias incredulously. "I've never even seen an elf."

Thorin nodded. "I've known at least a few in my time. It's not something that dwarves like to reveal. Half-lings are discriminated against at Mount Velik, although mageborn dwarves are highly esteemed."

"That doesn't make much sense—especially if you basically have to be a half-ling in order to be a dwarf mage."

"I didn't say there was any logic to it, boy. My people are long-lived and set in their ways. That's just the way things are. It takes a lot to change us." Thorin removed his pipe from his coat pocket and started to smoke.

Elias smelled the pungent smokeleaf in the air. His eyes started to get heavy. "Thorin, do you mind if I ask—how old are you?"

Thorin smiled and blew rings of smoke. "I'm not old by the standards of my people, but I'm old by human standards. Let's see... When your grandmother was a little girl, I was already a full-grown man. Does that help?"

"Really?" asked Elias, his eyes wide.

"Yes, really. Now go to sleep. We have a long day ahead of us tomorrow."

Elias pulled the hide around him and tried to get comfortable. His mind raced—*I've learned more about my family in the last week than I have my entire life. There's no way I'm going to be able to sleep,* he thought, but just moments later he drifted off.

Elias had been asleep for hours when the cold awoke him. He shivered and pulled the hide closer to his body. His crystal lay on the ground, still glowing dimly. Elias picked it up and saw that Thorin was asleep. That was odd. He was always good at covering the first watch.

I wonder how long we've both been sleeping, he thought to himself. It was pitch black. The sky was overcast and there were no moon or stars visible. It was impossible to estimate the hour.

A cold burst of wind hit him again, and he shivered. *I should probably let Thorin sleep. I can take over the watch.* Elias sat up and stretched. As he did so, he felt a clammy finger slide across the nape of his neck.

"Aughhh!" he screamed, spinning around.

"Ssssssso boy, we meet again," said the necromancer. She removed her cloak. In the dim light of the crystal, he could see the necromancer's milky white skin. Her eyes and hair were black, and she had no pupils.

Elias' face drained of color, and he felt blood pounding in his ears. "Thorin! Thorin! Wake up!" he yelled, but Thorin did not respond.

"Your dwarf friend cannot hear you. He's slumbering until I say otherwise." She floated over and patted Thorin on the head like a dog. "I could leave him ssssleeping for all eternity. Or at least until he starved to death," she hissed, laughing.

"W-What do you want?" asked Elias.

"Isn't it obvious, my boy? I want you. You're the reason I've come here. I'm going to take you back to the emperor myself. Why do you think I let you escape in Jutland?"

Elias gasped. "You were following us the whole time?"

The necromancer smiled, revealing rows of razor-sharp red teeth. "Sssssilly boy... Do you think your little spell was going to fool me? I sssssmelled you in that donkey cart before you even reached the gate." She laughed again, a bubbling cackle. "Your sssssspell was like that of a first-year mage."

"Why did you come all the way here to capture us?"

"I followed you here to capture *you*, boy. When I take you back to the emperor, he will grant me my freedom, and I can leave the capital forever. We necromancers are prisssssoners of the emperor, sssssubject to all of his brutalities and caprices." Then she smiled, and said, "You will buy me my *liberty*, boy!"

She grabbed Elias by his tunic and he screamed. Her hands were as cold as ice. Elias tried to cast a spell to free himself, but his mind went blank. He'd never felt so terrified in his entire life.

Just then, Thorin raised his head and snorted, "Humph! Not so fast, dark lady."

The necromancer spun around, "What? Impossible! You cannot have broken my sssspell!"

"You spellcasters always underestimate us dwarves. I always have a trick up my sleeve," said Thorin, smiling. "How much did the emperor tell you about this boy?"

The necromancer's black eyes narrowed. "Enough. That he needs to be returned to the capital alive. That is all I need to know. I follow my emperor's orders—nothing else is important."

"I beg to differ, dark one... this boy is Carina Dorgumir's grandson."

The necromancer inhaled sharply and released Elias' tunic. "No! It cannot be!"

"Yes, it is. Look into his eyes. You know it to be true."

The necromancer was stunned. Her mouth moved silently, her breath hissing past sharpened teeth, but she did not speak.

Now is my chance! Elias thought. "*Hringr-Incêndio!*" he cried, and a ball of flame appeared in his hand. He threw it at the startled necromancer, and it hit her squarely in the chest. It was a simple spell, but it caught the necromancer by surprise.

She shrieked, and her clothing burst into flames. She retreated back into the forest, screaming continuously.

The horses, startled by the noise, woke up. Elias ran over to Thorin and offered his hand. "Get up, Thorin. Let's get out of here!"

"I can't," he said. "I'm paralyzed from the neck down. Remember my pendant? It's also a protective amulet. It blocked part of the spell, but I have to wait until the necromancer releases me, or the spell wears off. Ye'll have to pick me up and sling me over Duster's saddle. If ye tie me into place, I can ride that way. It's almost dawn, so we'll be able to see well enough to ride."

"Okay, just as long as we get out of here. I got lucky with that fireball spell, but I doubt I'll be able to surprise her again." Elias grunted as he picked up Thorin. "Ugh! What a weight! You're shorter than me, but you weigh twice as much!"

"Aye, sorry," nodded Thorin. "We dwarves are a solid folk." Thorin seemed unperturbed by his current situation, and, in fact, was taking all of it in stride.

Elias quickly tied Thorin to Duster's saddle, and by the time he was finished pink light was visible on the horizon. Then he mounted Buttercup and dug his heels into her side, "Heyah, let's go!" They were off. Elias went as fast as they could with Thorin in his condition. Thorin never complained, even though his position was surely uncomfortable.

The sky cleared, and in the distance Elias could see the pale outline of Hwīt Rock.

His heart pounding, Elias thought, *Thorin was right. We've got to get out of this forest, or we're both going to die. I'm not stopping until we reach the river.*

The Elder Willow

It had been five days since Tallin and Duskeye left the safety of the Death Sands, and three days since the battle near Rignus. They traveled cautiously over the Elburgian Mountains and now they were entering Darkmouth Forest.

They'd slept in a cave at the forest's edge the previous evening and now were only traveling at night. The sun had set an hour ago, and Duskeye took flight with his rider. They both felt refreshed from their sleep.

"We should reach the Elder Willow by midnight," said Tallin. "Be prepared for anything."

Duskeye nodded. *I am ready, my friend.*

They both knew that this was the most dangerous part of the journey. They had to be prepared for a trap. Everything—the note, the spy, the stone—could be a trick. The emperor may have conceived this elaborate ruse, only to lure them away from the Death Sands and into the arms of death.

A yellow crescent moon hung in the sky, lighting their way. The moonlight cast spidery shadows across Duskeye's scarred wings. Tallin's hands were also covered in scars, a testament to his time under the emperor's torture.

Many years had passed, but Tallin never forgot what he had endured at the emperor's hands. During the Dragon Wars, Tallin and Duskeye were captured as prisoners of war. They suffered unimaginable cruelties. Tallin never broke his silence, but in the end Tallin suffered for nothing. All the other dragon riders bowed under torture. As soon as they revealed their secrets, the emperor slaughtered them and their dragons as well.

If the emperor was lucky enough to capture a dragon and a rider together, he killed the dragon first, and then the rider. If the emperor only captured one, he would shatter the dragon stone using necromancy and kill them both. The emperor tried to avoid using the second method, because shattering the dragon stone usually cost him the life of one of his necromancers, as well.

In the end, the emperor spared Tallin because he viewed him as a challenge. Vosper enjoyed torturing Tallin personally, and his torments grew more elaborate as time went on. But Vosper also became lazier at guarding Tallin.

Every day Tallin remained alive was another opportunity for escape. Eventually, one of Tallin's regular guards was replaced by a new guardsman for the afternoon. It was only for a short while, but it was enough. Tallin used the last of his strength to cast a concealment spell. The inexperienced guard thought that Tallin had escaped. The guard panicked, unlocked the cell door, and Tallin snapped his neck. Tallin switched the dead guard's clothing with his own and positioned the guard in the cell as a decoy.

Next he went searching for his dragon stone. He knew that he would never be able to find Duskeye without it. Tallin's dragon stone had been stolen from him when he was captured. It was an implant, so Vosper had ripped it out of Tallin's chest.

Tallin could sense the stone's presence, and he tracked it down in the castle. He eventually found the dragon stone in the armory, set into a cheap dagger and tossed in a pile with hundreds of other weapons. He approached the armory guard, and said, "I need a new knife. I lost mine two days ago when I was sparring."

The guard nodded, and picked out a nice dagger from the collection. "Here you go. This is a sturdy one."

Tallin pretended to examine it for cracks. "Nah, I don't like the grip on this one. How about that one over there, the one with the blue stone in the hilt?" Tallin cleared his throat and pointed at the dagger with the dragon stone.

"You don't want that one—it's a piece of garbage. It's bronze and tin."

"Let me see it," insisted Tallin.

"All right, but I promise you, it's rubbish."

The guard handed Tallin the knife, handle first. As soon as Tallin touched the stone, he felt power rushing back into his body. He closed his eyes, and the armory guard asked, "Hey, are you all right, mate?"

"Yes, yes," answered Tallin, recovering his composure. "This one will do fine, thank you."

The armory guard shook his head and waved him off. "Take it then, but don't come back complaining after the blade breaks."

"Thanks," said Tallin, walking away. He was already prying the dragon stone from the hilt. He had no idea why or how the dragon stone ended up in the armory, but he was thankful. Tallin had always used his dragon stone to store energy. Each time he touched it, waves of energy flooded back into his weakened body. With the stone in his possession, he also was able to feel Duskeye—badly injured but alive, deep below the castle in Vosper's cavernous dungeons.

Still in disguise, Tallin ran down to the caverns below the castle. There were two guards at the entrance, and Tallin walked by them quietly.

"I'm down here checking on a prisoner for the captain," he said.

The guards allowed him to pass without incident. His anger built up inside, but fighting these men would take energy that he couldn't spare. In order to heal Duskeye, he knew he would have to save his strength.

The conditions in the dungeons were deplorable. The smell of rotting flesh was overwhelming, and he vomited. Tallin sensed Duskeye at the edge of his consciousness—his friend was at the brink of death. "Hold on, my friend!" Tallin said, trying to communicate with Duskeye. There was no response. The dragon was too weak.

Tallin continued to walk deeper into the caves, and the stench increased. Partially decomposed corpses, still chained to the walls, softened and putrefied next to prisoners who were still alive. The smell of mold, straw, and something much worse... as Tallin walked farther, he came upon an open fire pit. A man wrapped in chains was hanging above it. He had been cooked. Tallin shuddered, but continued to walk. Finally, he found Duskeye, chained by the neck to a brick wall. His feet were also immobilized with chains. The chains were so short that they prevented him from turning his body. He couldn't even lie down. Duskeye's bones poked through the skin, and many of his scales were missing. A shattered right leg hung limply to the side. Worst of all, his wings had been flayed and hung in limp strips. They were unusable. It was worse than Tallin imagined. Would his dragon ever fly again?

Tallin walked over to his companion, tears streaming down his face. One of the dragon's eyes fluttered open. The other was sealed shut, swollen and caked with blood.

Tallin...my old friend, said Duskeye, weakly. *I knew you were still alive. It was the only thing that gave me the strength to keep going.*

"I swear upon my life, I will never leave your side again. We're going to get out of here," said Tallin.

I cannot fly, my friend. I cannot walk. My body is broken. Take my dragon stone. I will surrender it to you so that you may live. Join both halves and save yourself.

"We're leaving here together. A life without you is no life at all." Tallin reached his hand out and touched Duskeye's crushed limb. *"Curatio!"*

Tallin's hands began to glow, and underneath his palm he felt Duskeye's bones knit back together. Duskeye groaned in pain.

Tallin fell to one knee, exhausted by the simple effort. He touched the dragon stone again, leeching more of its precious energy. His reserves were depleted, but the stone might hold enough energy to save them both. "There. Can you walk?"

Duskeye moved his leg gingerly, and then touched the ground with his foot. *I can put weight on it.* It was weak, but he could walk with a limp. His skin still looked terrible, but at least the bones were healed. *Let us go. I can walk.*

Tallin's humble spell was a triumph, and it would allow them to escape.

"We must hurry!"

Do not worry, my friend. The guards come down here only rarely. I have not been fed for a long time.

"That's actually good news for us. We may have more time to plan our escape from this abyss. I left a decoy in my cell. If we're fortunate, we'll have a day to escape."

It has been two days since I've seen the emperor's torturer. The last time he paid a visit, he ignored me and strung that poor wretch above the fire pit. Duskeye pointed at the corpse. *Vosper came down here himself. He smiled and watched the man scream for about an hour. Then he left him here to roast over the fire. The prisoner screamed for hours before he died.*

"This place is the very heart of evil," said Tallin.

After unlocking Duskeye's shackles, they hobbled into the caves underneath the castle and hid. Tallin spent

182

the night healing Duskeye's tattered wings. Tallin worked all night, drawing energy from the dragon stone and from his meager reserves. By the next morning, Duskeye's wings were healed enough to fly short distances. Tallin was an accomplished mage before he was captured, but escaping the castle tested his abilities to their limit. It was two days before the emperor noticed that Tallin was missing, but by then, they were gone. Duskeye flew small distances as he could, and Tallin cast a spell to camouflage them whenever there was a chance they could be seen.

The emperor sent necromancers out to search for them, but Tallin used elaborate spells to conceal them. They also zigzagged across the land, choosing a less obvious route. Afraid to trust anyone, they traveled only at night, slowly making their way across Durn to the Death Sands. They knew it was the only place where they could be safe. They survived by scavenging through the countryside. They ate rats, grubs, and when they were lucky, stolen livestock. A month later, they finally reached the Death Sands where they hid. They told no one about their escape or their location, even other dragon riders.

It took them a year to physically recover from their ordeal. Their wounds healed, but the emotional scars would last forever.

Tallin—Tallin, are you woolgathering again? Duskeye asked.

"Just thinking about old times, my friend."

As always. We're nearly there.

"Right. I am ready."

Tallin raised his hands, and the air shimmered around them. The Elder Willow came into view. In the moonlight, the tree was clearly visible. It was magnificent.

The Elder Willow was massive, knotted, with branches reaching out hundreds of feet. As they approached, an angry tree sprite buzzed forward. It was ugly, small, and greenish, with a long nose. Its white hair was tangled in countless knots. The sprite had clear wings, which were shaped like a butterfly's, but larger. It flew up to Tallin and Duskeye, but it did not attempt to harm them. If Tallin had been human, the sprite could have attacked him with thorns, bees, or some minor spell.

Tallin waved it off. "Shoo! Stop bothering us, you little pest."

The sprite scowled, crossing its arms. It hovered around Tallin, watching his movements. Eventually, the sprite circled Duskeye's head and kicked the dragon with its little foot. Duskeye flicked his tongue out and licked the sprite, which surprised the little creature. It flew back to the willow and disappeared among the branches.

Do you sense anything here? asked Duskeye. He got on all fours and circled the tree.

"No. Only the magic of the forest. Perhaps our trip has been wasted."

They sat for a minute, thinking about what they should do next.

"Well, if someone is hiding here, they wouldn't have made it that easy for us, would they? Maybe there's a riddle we have to solve."

The sprite came down from the branches and pointed to a knot in the tree. Tallin felt inside and pulled out a flat stone. It was white, flat, and as smooth as glass.

"So, what do you think, old friend?"

Let me see it. Tallin held up the stone, and Duskeye cocked his head so he could examine it with his good eye. *It looks like a runestone. We just have to figure out how to unlock it.*

"I haven't seen a white runestone in ages. I've seen quite a few black ones though. And recently. They're used for black magic. Lazy spellcasters use them because they can set a charm within the stone and leave it. But you can never guarantee who is going to pick it up, so it's a very imprecise way to set a trap. The first time I saw one, it was during my first year of study at Aonach. The black ones can be nasty, so I just left it where I found it."

The white ones can be nasty, too. Don't they usually cause amnesia?

"Yes. But it's better than the black ones. A black runestone usually causes death."

Tallin stared at the stone for a moment, turning it over in his palm. "*Pārēre!*" he said, and the stone began to glow. Carved runes appeared on its surface. It was another riddle:

I am forever hungry,
I must be fed,
Feed me and I live,
Water me and I die.

"That old chestnut? The answer is fire. I learned that riddle when I was a child," said Tallin. "Now, what completes the riddle?"

Tallin, I think we need to decide what we're going to do... and fast, said Duskeye.

Tallin looked up and saw a swarm filling the sky. It was hundreds of tree sprites, all coming to the Elder Willow. They were gathering to defend it. As they touched down, he heard their wings buzzing like the sound of a thousand bees. They glowed like fireflies.

While a single sprite was simply annoying, a dozen sprites could easily kill a man, and a hundred of them could kill even an experienced mage like Tallin. Their magic was raw, erratic, and capricious. Sprites were powerful in numbers because their power was virtually unlimited—they collected their strength from the forest itself. The noise was deafening, and Tallin's ears started to burn.

"By Baghra, this doesn't look good. We've got to get out of here!"

Can we fight them? asked Duskeye.

"There's no way that we could kill them all. There are hundreds, maybe thousands. We've got to figure this out, now!"

Tallin, I've got an idea. Throw the stone in the air.

Tallin complied, and dragon's fire erupted from Duskeye's mouth, showering the stone with white flame. The stone burst apart midair, like a popped acorn, revealing a glowing key.

"Grab it!" said Tallin.

Duskeye reached down and flipped the key to Tallin with his tongue. The sprites were circling around them now, throwing rocks, pebbles, and thorns. Tallin started to feel sick. He reached back into the knothole and felt to the bottom. There was a keyhole. He inserted the key just in time—the base of the tree opened up, revealing a passage that had not been visible before.

"Let's get out of here!" screamed Tallin, and they squeezed through the opening. The sprites swarmed angrily around them, but did not follow them into the tree. Once they had entered the passage, the opening slammed shut behind them. They stood in darkness, so Duskeye produced a tiny flame from his nostrils to light the way.

The passage became a tunnel, lined with tree roots, winding deep underground. "I can't see the end of it. We're just going to have to walk down and hope for the best. Keep your guard up," warned Tallin.

The corridor was narrow, and Duskeye's back scraped the ceiling in some areas. After a few minutes, they came to a larger room. It was as silent as a tomb.

Something's here, said Duskeye.

"I know. I can feel it, too. Give us a little more light."

Duskeye opened his mouth, and the light flared.

There, lying in the corner of the room, sitting quietly in the dark, was Starclaw. Her faded emerald scales glittered in the firelight. And to her left sat her rider, Chua, the fallen one. Tallin stepped closer—and gasped.

The dragon and her rider stared ahead with eyeless sockets. Gaping holes remained where their eyes had once been. And there was more. Chua sat under a blanket, but Tallin could see that his legs had been severed. Starclaw stood up, and as she did so, her wings unfurled. Her right wing was almost completely gone; it had been torn off at the shoulder. Duskeye shuddered. A dragon that could not fly or see? What kind of travesty was this?

They were alive, but horribly disfigured. Tallin and Duskeye stood mute with shock. Even after what he had endured in the emperor's dungeons, Tallin knew that this was the worst he had ever seen.

And then Starclaw spoke. *Please, dragon friend... and rider... come and sit with us. We have much to discuss.*

The Orvasse River

The sun was setting by the time Thorin and Elias arrived at Hwīt Rock. They had to stop frequently because Thorin kept falling off the saddle. Eventually, the necromancer's spell began to wear off, and Thorin got back the use of his arms. It took them twice as long to reach the river as Thorin had originally predicted. That meant it would be more difficult finding passage up the river.

The outpost was a bustle of activity. Merchants, travelers, traders, and peasants filled the streets. It was a small trading post, but a prosperous one. The streets were clean and well-maintained, and private guards patrolled the riverbanks on horseback. The guards examined Elias and Thorin impassively. They were alert, but calm.

"Thorin, this is a nice place," remarked Elias, watching the sailboats coming and going.

"Yes, the magistrate that runs this outpost is an honest man. People know that when they come here for goods, they won't get cheated."

"So...it's basically the opposite of Faerroe."

Thorin laughed. "Yes, I suppose it is. I don't see any empire soldiers. We can probably relax a little bit now. Let's grab somethin' to eat from one of the street vendors. I'm dyin' for a hot meal."

Elias nodded in agreement. They hadn't stopped to eat all day, so he was starving. "I'll eat anything. I have a few coppers. Do you think that will be enough?"

"Don't you worry about that, lad. I've got problems just like everyone else, but money isn't one of them." Thorin pulled a little pouch from underneath his beard, and he shook out a silver coin. "This should be enough to get us a nice meal and some provisions for the trip."

He handed the coin to Elias. It had been years since he'd held so much money in his hands. "Thank you. I'm good at haggling at the market. My grandmother taught me how to do it without being embarrassed. She even let me sell herbs on my own. What should I buy?"

"Buy us some hot sausages for dinner; they're excellent here. And see if you can find some dried meat. They sell lamb jerky inside the fort. It's available year round. Go in and ask for *quadid.* That's my favorite, and it's the local specialty. The food vendors are all outside, and ye'll find at least two or three. Buy some sausage wrapped in black bread—it's hot and delicious." Thorin patted his stomach and licked his lips.

"Okay. Where are you going?"

"I'll be on the docks looking for Gremley and the Chipperwick. Hopefully he's here. He's trustworthy—I've used him before. Either way, though, we need to find passage up the river tonight. Go ahead and hand me Buttercup's reins. You won't be able to take your horse inside the outpost.

"Remember, if anyone asks, your name is 'Barth,' and you're from Faerroe. I'll meet you back here within the hour." The dwarf trotted off, still riding Duster. Elias wondered if Thorin was able to use his legs yet. Thorin didn't seem bothered by it either way.

Elias walked towards the outpost, which was built entirely from rough-hewn logs. Outside, green ivy climbed the walls, and there were local militia patrolling the docks. It was so busy that merchants spilled out onto the dock. Inside the outpost, there were dozens of tiny shops, with hundreds of people selling and buying goods.

On the right, one man sold furs. The next vendor sold hunting weapons. A third sold dried herbs and other medicines. It was an apothecary shop. Elias couldn't hide his curiosity, and he walked up, touching the familiar medicines. The shopkeeper slapped his hand away. "Don't touch, boy! These're fer payin' customers only!"

"I have money," said Elias, defiantly, pulling out his coin pouch. "I can pay—and if you want to sell to me, you'd *better* give me a good price."

"Let me see it then," said the man.

Elias showed the merchant his silver coin, and the apothecary leered, rubbing his hands together. "Ah, many apologies, young master. What pleases you this fine day?"

"I want two drams of dried gingerroot, a bottle of feverfew elixir, and a tincture of hyssop," said Elias. These would come in handy while they were traveling.

"Sure, boy, I'll get those ready for you. It will be a few minutes."

"I'll be back then. I need to buy some other supplies," Elias replied.

He found two vendors selling cooked sausage outside. One sold venison and the other sold lamb. He haggled with both men to see which would give him the best price, and he was able to get a nice helping of each. Then he purchased some dried lamb.

A short while later, he walked back to the herbalist's booth and asked, "Is my order ready?"

"Yes, I have it right here." The herbalist lifted a parcel. "That will be seven coppers."

"Seven coppers! That's robbery," said Elias. "Those herbs would cost no more than three coppers in Persil!"

"Persil?" The merchant's eyes opened wide. "Is that where you're from, boy?"

Elias stepped back, stuttering. "No. I-I—I'm from Faerroe."

The man stepped closer to him, squinting his eyes. He had said too much.

"What is your *name*, boy?" People were starting to stare.

"B-Barth. My name's Barth," Elias lied, inching his way back towards the entrance.

"Are you *sure*, boy? Are you sure your name isn't... *Elias?*" screeched the man, pointing at the wall. Elias gasped. There was a reward poster with his likeness pinned above the entrance. The reward was one hundred gold crowns! *I have to get out of here!* he thought to himself. He spun, tucking the sausages into his tunic, and ran.

"Stop! Stop that boy! Stop him!" yelled the shopkeeper, while leaping forward to grab Elias' tunic. The shopkeeper missed, landing face-first into the dirt. Elias sprinted all the way to the dock and found Thorin waiting by a robust sailboat. The necromancer's spell had worn off—Thorin was walking on his own. Their horses were being led on board by the ship's captain. The captain was a bearded man, tall and muscular, with skin like a burnt chestnut.

Elias ran towards Thorin on the docks. Thorin noticed him, and waved him on the boat. "Ah, there ye are—welcome to the Chipperwick! The captain's name is Gremley. I know him from way back. He's agreed to transport us to Ironport. The horses are already on board, so we were just waiting for ye."

Gremley nodded and said, "Aye. Get on board, son, and we'll be off." He wasn't a man of many words.

Elias leaned in and whispered frantically, "Thorin, we've got to get the heck out of here! One of the shopkeepers recognized me! There's a reward poster on the wall inside the outpost, with a drawing of my face!"

Thorin frowned, saying quietly, "That is bad news, indeed. It's a shame, but we can't do nothin' for it. They're lookin' for ye, and ye'll just have to be more careful." Thorin cleared his throat, and said loudly, "Ah, Barth! It's a shame ye don't feel well, my boy! I think it's best that ye go below and lay down." Thorin patted Elias' back and directed him into the hold below.

Then Thorin turned to Gremley and said, "He's got a bit o' delicate stomach."

Gremley just snorted in response. He untied the ropes holding the boat to the dock, and moments later they were off. Elias hurried down the steps and crouched down in the ship's hold. He heard Gremley and Thorin stomping back and forth on deck, and soon after, the ship was moving.

Elias peered out the filthy porthole and saw the herbalist running back and forth on the dock. He was gesturing frantically at the guards and shaking his hands above his head. Elias was frightened.

Thorin came down and whispered, "Don't worry, my boy. We'll be fine. There's at least twenty boats comin' and goin' right now, and it's already gettin' dark."

"It was horrible, Thorin. Everyone was looking at me like I was a criminal... I'm not safe anywhere, am I?"

"Maybe not right now, but ye'll be safe at Mount Velik. We just have to get ye there in one piece, is all."

Elias smiled. Then he remembered the sausages. He pulled them out of his cloak, handing one to Thorin. "Here's the lamb sausage. I got some venison, too."

"Ah, good job, boy—this will hit the spot! Eat fast, though—I don't want Gremley to see ye swallowin' a huge meal right after I told him that ye were stomach-sick."

Elias chuckled, and ate quickly. Thorin always made him feel better. It was probably because he was so calm all the time. After they finished eating, Elias felt tired. He lay down on clean straw.

"Get some rest, boy. I'm goin' back on deck to speak with Gremley. I'll see if he has any news of the empire."

"How about you? Aren't you going to sleep?"

"Boy, I've just spent the entire day paralyzed and strapped to a saddle. I'll enjoy walkin' around for a while."

Elias smiled and drifted off to sleep. Thorin went back up to the deck and watched the water. The river was full of merchant ships, transporting goods up and down the countryside. It was an efficient system, and the Orvasse River was the busiest waterway on Durn. He breathed the fresh air, and then sat down to smoke his pipe quietly.

"Is the boy asleep?" asked Gremley.

"Aye. He was feelin' a bit nauseated is all," replied Thorin.

"Let him sleep. The weather is calm, and I expect it to be quiet," said Gremley. "Thorin, I saw the posters inside the fort. Is this the boy they're lookin' for?"

"Honestly...yes. It is him. It's my job to get him to safety. Any chance we'll be able to get past Morholt without being noticed? The emperor wants this boy very badly."

Gremley shrugged. "It's possible, if we're careful. If you're tryin' to get past Morholt with smuggled goods, it's near impossible these days. They're lookin' for every possible reason to confiscate your goods. The emperor is stealing from his own people in order to finance his latest war. Empire soldiers search almost every ship."

"I know. We've had a few encounters with empire soldiers already, and they haven't been pleasant."

"I could probably conceal the boy," said Gremley, "but if the emperor has necromancers watching the shoreline, then you've got a serious problem."

"Well, hopefully we won't see any necromancers. Thank you for taking us, Gremley. I hoped that I would find ye here, but I wasn't sure until I saw ye standin' on the docks. We haven't even stopped to rest. I don't know if we would have escaped without yer help."

"Happy to be of service. I'm no friend of the empire, but you're takin' a mighty big risk by harboring this boy. You're lucky that you didn't cross paths with any necromancers, or the boy would have been taken captive for sure."

"Actually—we did cross paths with a necromancer. In Jutland. It allowed us to leave the city, only to follow us all the way through Darkmouth Forest. It confronted us a day ago."

The captain was incredulous. "You were attacked by a necromancer—and you lived? He's just a child, and you don't have any powers. How did you both survive?"

"Just lucky, I guess. Gremley, do you know anything about the old myths?"

"Some. I heard stories during the Dragon Wars when I was a soldier. That was many years ago."

"Well, the prophesy says that the emperor will be defeated by a new dragon rider. I believe this boy is the one. It's my job to get him to Mount Velik alive."

"Thorin, you're a crazy old dwarf, but your money is good. I can't make any guarantees, but I'll do my best to get you both to safety. I have no love for the emperor, so as long as I can help you, I will," said Gremley.

"I appreciate that, friend," said Thorin.

Thorin looked up at the night sky. This had been an interesting week, indeed. The dragon stone appeared, then the boy, and that necromancer! Things had not been this chaotic since the Dragon War.

It was rare enough to see a female necromancer, but this one had looked strikingly familiar. Thorin had a hunch in Jutland, but when the necromancer appeared again in the forest, his gut feeling was confirmed.

The undead creature that attacked them in Darkmouth Forest was Ionela.

He was sure of it—that necromancer was Elias' mother.

****

Continued in Book Two: The Return of the Dragon Riders

About the Author

Kristian Alva was born into a family of writers and teachers. She worked as a staff writer and a ghostwriter before publishing her own manuscripts. She now writes young adult and middle-grade fantasy full-time.

She currently lives in California with her husband and son. When she's not writing, she enjoys reading all genres, especially epic fantasy. Find out more about the author at her official website: *www.KristianAlva.com.*

Printed in Great Britain
by Amazon.co.uk, Ltd.,
Marston Gate.